A dark shape froze as her eyes found it.

Darby scanned the shade under the candlenut tree. That's where there'd been motion, then stillness.

There! Starlight showed her a swath of gleaming blackness.

Determined to find out if her imagination was running amok, Darby took a large step off the porch.

The horse exploded from cover.

Darby heard hide scrape tree bark. She smelled soil and leaves dug up by hooves. A whirlwind snatched Darby's hair and waved the ends against her cheeks.

She heard it. She felt it. She even smelled hot horseflesh. But she didn't see a thing.

Check out the

Phantom Stallion

series, also by Terri Farley!

Phantom Stallion

WILD HORSE ISLAND 2

THE SHINING STALLION

TERRI FARLEY

HarperTrophy®
An Imprint of HarperCollins*Publishers*

Harper Trophy® is a registered trademark of HarperCollins Publishers.

The Shining Stallion
Copyright © 2007 by Terri Sprenger-Farley

Library of Congress Catalog Card Number: 2007925201
ISBN 978-0-06-081543-1

Typography by Jennifer Heuer
❖
First Harper Trophy edition, 2007

Read all the **Phantom Stallion** WILD HORSE ISLAND *adventures!*

Thanks to Billy Bergin, President of the Paniolo Preservation Society, who heard hooves in the night

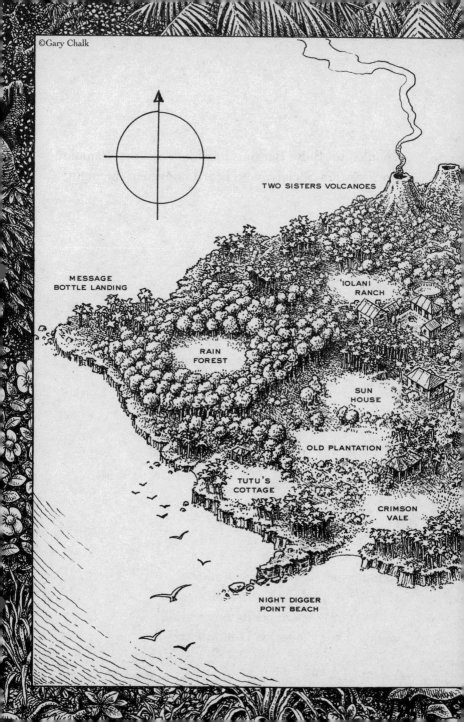

©Gary Chalk

TWO SISTERS VOLCANOES

MESSAGE
BOTTLE LANDING

'IOLANI
RANCH

RAIN
FOREST

SUN
HOUSE

OLD PLANTATION

TUTU'S
COTTAGE

CRIMSON
VALE

NIGHT DIGGER
POINT BEACH

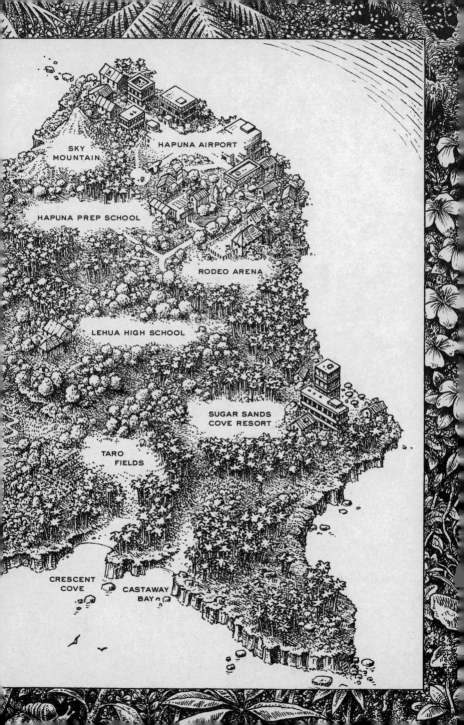

2
THE SHINING STALLION

Chapter 1

The girl and horse stood nose to nose.

Trade winds swirled the scents of trees and cinnamon-red dirt around them. Truck tires crunched on the rough road to 'Iolani Ranch, a goat's bleat mixed with birdsong, and the harsh neigh of a stallion rang out from a distant pasture.

But the girl only noticed her horse's hay-sweet breath and the flick of her flattened ears. Darby smiled at Hoku's determination to win their stare-off.

She'd named the filly Hoku, the Hawaiian word for *star*, after the white marking on her chest, but Darby Carter couldn't help comparing the young horse to something else.

Nitroglycerine, Darby thought as she stepped

toward her golden-red filly. One wrong move could make that chemical explode.

Darby scuffed her boots in the dirt. She couldn't move any closer without ramming into the filly, but Hoku didn't know that.

The sorrel braced her legs and tossed her mane. Her stare stabbed past strands of ivory forelock.

Friendship was one thing. Giving in to a halter was something else.

Hoku would never be truly tame. Darby knew that haltering her mustang was about as safe as playing with explosives.

"Hey, good girl, don't look so worried," Darby said.

Hoku vibrated with a silent nicker and her head rose an inch. For a second, Darby felt as if they were the only two creatures on the island, but then Hoku glanced over Darby's shoulder, through the corral rails, and glared at their audience.

"Stay close."

Darby didn't turn at Cade's voice. His eyes tracked her moves, but he wasn't adding up her mistakes. He was keeping her under surveillance for her own good.

Not that Cade and everyone else on 'Iolani Ranch thought she was insane, but she'd understand if they did. To say she'd made a few big mistakes last week was an understatement. She'd given new meaning to the term *horse crazy*.

"But I've learned my lesson, haven't I, pretty girl," Darby said.

Hoku's eyes widened in curiosity as Darby sauntered around to the horse's left side.

Darby and Cade had been talking since dawn about how to halter the head-shy filly. Staying close, without doing anything Hoku found scary, was the first step.

Once, a man had tried to beat the filly's wild horse wariness out of her. It hadn't worked. Hoku's spirit matched her fiery gold coat. She hated men and she didn't like anyone, even Darby, touching her head.

"Exhale," Darby whispered to herself. Hoku shouldn't feel tension quaking off her.

After three quiet breaths, Darby leaned her shoulder against Hoku's.

The filly didn't shift away. Instead, she rearranged her front hooves to return the gentle pressure.

"Perfect." Darby barely breathed the word before raising her arms in a hug and rubbing the filly's poll.

At last Hoku relaxed. Her head drooped until her lips were even with Darby's knees.

Now came the hard part. Could she tie a soft rope halter on Hoku's lowered head?

"Stay close," Cade repeated.

Darby guessed she should have given some sign that she'd heard him the first time, but after all, shouldn't a horseman like Cade know she didn't want to set off Hoku by having a conversation with him?

Cade had studied the way of Hawaii's cowboys, the *paniolo*, and he was apprenticed to her grandfather Jonah, a man known as the Hawaiian horse charmer.

"Hear me?" Cade asked.

Darby risked a tiny nod. That was all it took to detonate the filly's wildness.

Hoku bolted into a gallop. Strides meant to cross an endless range took her around and around the corral.

Darby kept herself from groaning, but her arm had a mind of its own. It flung the orange rope halter down in frustration.

Hoku's front legs lifted. Her hooves jounced down as if the halter was a snake and she wanted to pound the life out of it. Then, Hoku wheeled and raced in the opposite direction.

"Your temper just set you back an hour," Cade pointed out, but she still didn't look at him.

She knew what she'd see: brown eyes set in a sun-browned face beneath a brown luahala hat that hid the only spot of color about him, the tight blond braid of a *paniolo*.

Squinting her eyes against the dust swirling around her, Darby snatched up the halter. She sorted it back into shape by touch, without taking her eyes off Hoku.

Reversing her morning's progress, Darby backed toward the fence until she collided with it.

"Go away. Please."

"Jonah wants me to supervise—"

"But—"

"And he's the boss," Cade finished.

Wishing she could communicate with Cade as well as she could with Hoku, Darby considered the hand-me-down boots she'd accepted from Megan Kato, the ranch manager's daughter. Scuffed through the reddish finish of the oxblood leather, they were real cowgirl boots and Darby loved them, but they didn't supply any ideas on how to convince Cade she needed to be alone with her horse.

"We'll be okay," Darby promised, and when Cade didn't contradict her, she slid her eyes around far enough to see that he was staring up at the pillowy gray clouds.

"Suppose it's this storm that's got Luna so spooky?" Cade asked her, and Darby heard the stallion neighing from the lower pastures again, though he was usually quiet during the day.

"It doesn't look like much," Darby said. She hadn't been in Hawaii long, but the clouds didn't look like they were holding a downpour that would send her scurrying inside to curl up on her bed with a book. "Maybe you should go check on him."

Cade's second silence had to mean a weakening in his resolve.

"Maybe I will," Cade said. "Something's got him stirred up." He pushed back from the fence so abruptly, the post joint creaked with a sound like a starter's gun. "Be right back."

Yes! Cade's retreat worked like magic. As the boy turned away, Hoku slowed to a jog, then a walk. Then she stopped, sneezing at the dust halo she'd raised.

"Hoku," Darby said brightly as if she hadn't seen her horse for days, and the filly watched Darby tighten her black ponytail. "Here's what I think. We need to stop worrying about what Shan Stonerow did to you and get on with our lives."

When the sorrel sidestepped, Darby decided that "getting on with life" wasn't a concept a horse could grasp.

"I know," Darby sympathized. "He was a bad guy. He hit you in the face, but that won't ever happen again."

Darby closed her eyes, trying to send the filly an image of snow melting off the range, of warmth replacing cold.

"We're starting over, like springtime."

Darby stood close enough to touch Hoku's withers. She lifted her hand slowly and stroked the filly's golden mane. She crumpled it between her fingers, imitating the way horses groomed each other with gentle bites.

"We were making such good progress before you escaped. We can do it again."

Hoku shook her mane. She swung her head around to look at Darby. Her neck wrinkled like satin from all Darby's brushing, but her eyes questioned the girl.

Holding the halter's nosepiece open with her left hand, Darby inched her right arm higher, to ease the loose end of the headstall into position. When Hoku didn't move away, Darby delighted in the circle she made with her horse.

Hoku nudged the treat pouch Darby carried around her waist.

"Why yes, I do have hay for good little mustangs," she told Hoku. Darby slipped the nosepiece around Hoku's nose as the filly's agile lips worked at the pouch flap. "You love hay, don't you?"

Darby heard the scuff of boots behind her, but she concentrated on getting the loose end of rope through the loop over Hoku's poll. All she had to do now was tie it.

She knotted the rope.

That doesn't look right, she thought, but Hoku would lose interest if she didn't taste hay. Right now.

Darby drew her hands back slowly, as if balancing. The halter stayed on.

She unsnapped the treat pouch and Hoku snatched a mouthful of hay. She gave a single chomp before swallowing, then nudged Darby for more. The sorrel didn't back away until she'd eaten every stalk of hay and licked Darby's hand for traces she'd missed.

"Ta da!" Darby announced, turning to Cade.

Except that it wasn't Cade. It was Kit Ely, foreman of 'Iolani Ranch.

"Good work." He flashed Darby a smile, which looked extra white in the shade of his black Stetson.

Then, looking down to make an unneeded adjustment to his short leather chaps—Darby thought he called them *chinks*—Kit said, "Kinda wonder why you didn't snap on the lead rope while ya had her."

Darby looked at the tangerine-and-white-striped rope lying in the dirt nearby and sighed. "Me too."

She swiped a raindrop off her cheek, then bent inch by inch to gather up the rope.

Darby heard Hoku's mane flip from side to side as she shook her head.

Darby's fingers closed over the rope. Straightening slowly, she saw the orange halter fall off Hoku's head.

"I guess I didn't tie it right," Darby muttered.

Hoku snorted and gave a triumphant buck.

"You'll get it, Darby." Kit's voice was as encouraging as a pat on the back. "It just takes time."

Darby wasn't sure when Kit left and Cade returned, but after a long time of coaxing and feeding Hoku more hay, she managed to rehalter the filly.

Attaching the lead rope was another story. Hoku ran and bucked, kicked and squealed, until Cade told Darby it was time to give up.

"She almost got a hoof through her cheek piece that time. Better call it a day."

"Okay," Darby agreed, then remembered why Cade had left. "Is Luna okay?"

She felt almost silly asking after the stallion. The big bay ruled this ranch, but to Darby, every horse here was a miracle.

"I don't know what's gotten into him," Cade said, shooting a glance at Hoku.

What did that *mean?* Darby wondered as Cade walked toward the tack room.

He glanced over his shoulder to see her safely through the gate as it closed between her and Hoku.

By then it was raining steadily, but Darby still didn't want to leave her horse.

She felt good about their progress. After all, she and the filly had only been in Hawaii for two weeks.

Darby's horse-handling skills were improving, even though she was working toward a goal she didn't want to reach.

Once Darby could halter and lead Hoku without trouble, Jonah would exile them to the rain forest. Raised in the urban web of Southern California freeways, Darby was scared of the jungle.

But how bad could it be? She was in paradise, surrounded by horses, and one of them belonged to her!

As if Hoku hadn't had enough of Darby, either, the filly pressed against the fence. Darby rested her hand on Hoku's neck. The smooth curve of muscle beneath the sorrel's skin was no longer hot from injury. It slid beneath Darby's palm as the filly walked off to drop her nose into her water bucket.

"Hey," Darby said, grinning. "Isn't she doing great?" When Cade faced her, he nodded, but she noticed his jaw kind of shifted to one side.

Would she have noticed that ill-at-ease movement if Cade's jaw hadn't shown signs of being broken and healing sloppily?

Something was wrong. And now that she was outside the corral, Darby felt shy again.

Darby eased the collar of her blue shirt away from her neck. She wiped the back of her hand over her rain-wet forehead. And waited.

"Jonah wants to see you," Cade said.

Of course he did. She'd been silly to think Jonah would ignore last week's poor judgment.

"He said he'd be in his library," Cade said.

"I don't remember seeing it," Darby said. She reviewed the house's floor plan in her mind.

She was new to the ranch, and there hadn't been a lot of time for exploring. Still, she should have remembered a room full of books.

Cade could tell her how to find it, though. He was Jonah's foster son, and took classes by correspondence, so he must get to use Jonah's library.

Cade nodded toward Sun House. "Walk into the living room, yeah? And before you get to the lanai, call out for Jonah."

"Thanks," she said to Cade, then headed for the house, eager to get this showdown over.

Darby thought she totally deserved some kind of

punishment, but she had brought her horse home safely. That must count for a lot. Of course, while freeing Hoku had been an accident, slipping away from Megan after the older girl had helped her search for her wild horse hadn't been. Megan had made an effort at friendship and Darby had paid her back by getting her in trouble.

At least no one had asked for details of her sea crossing with Hoku. That was lucky, because they both could have drowned, and Darby still couldn't explain how she and Hoku had found their way back to 'Iolani Ranch in the dark.

But today was the day she found out what kind of disciplinarian her grandfather was, and how she'd handle punishment from someone besides her mother.

"For some reason I'm not that scared," Darby told the pack of Australian shepherds escorting her to the house.

With waving tails, merry eyes, and openmouthed leaps, they acted as if nothing bad would happen.

"Just the same, I don't take predictions from dogs," she told them. "No offense."

 Chapter 2

Darby sat on the low bench in Sun House's entrance hall and tugged off her boots. Her skinned knees were stiff from her fall down the boulders in Crimson Vale, but getting her boots off wasn't hard. Megan's outgrown boots were still a bit big for Darby and slid off easily.

Sitting in her stockinged feet, Darby gazed out the open front door. She didn't want to close it.

How could it feel more dreary inside the house than it did outside in the rain?

Because I'm going to my doom, Darby thought, but as she stood, she pushed the cuff of her long-sleeved T-shirt up to look at her good-luck charm.

It was all Samantha Forster's fault, Darby

decided. The Nevada cowgirl wore a bracelet braided from silvery strands of mustang mane. The idea had stuck with Darby. So even though she was not the least bit superstitious, when she'd found this ornament of three tiny black braids, which looked like a broken horsehair necklace, she hadn't been able to resist wrapping it around her wrist.

Darby didn't believe in good-luck charms. Tugging her sleeve back down, she thought maybe it couldn't hurt.

A thump drew her attention to the corner of the living room. The lowest of the wooden cabinets to the left of the lanai doors swung open.

Darby couldn't believe her eyes. Framed in the open cabinet, like a face on a television, was her grandfather's head.

"The entrance to my library's down here."

Darby felt like Alice in Wonderland as she asked, "Down where?"

She tilted her head to look inside. There were no shelves, no clutter of stored Christmas lights or old videos, only Jonah, crawling backward, away from her, deeper into a cabinet that had no back.

It was a secret door.

Disbelieving, Darby remained squatting.

Jonah's face reappeared. "Crawl in," he told her.

"Okay," Darby whispered.

"It's not that kind of library," Jonah told her. "Speak up."

"Okay." She walked her hands out in front of her until she was on all fours. "Here I come," she said, raising her voice.

From polished wooden floor to pillows, she crawled past Jonah. He closed the door behind her, but Darby didn't stop crawling until she'd reached the far wall. Then, twisting to sit, she cautiously raised her head to look around. Once you got through the entrance, there was room to stand, but Darby didn't.

Jonah's library wasn't much bigger than a closet, but full bookshelves were set in a spiral that started at floor level, then circled the room up to the ceiling. It was like being inside a shell.

Darby tilted her head back and saw that the bookshelves spiraled all the way up to an arched skylight.

"This is so cool," she gasped.

Arms and legs folded, Jonah sat back against the closed door, looking comfortable.

He shrugged at her delight, but a smile lifted his black mustache.

"What is it? I mean, I know it's your library, but—"

"I was a sickly little kid, like you," Jonah said. "Once I had to stay a week in the hospital, off island. When I came home, my dad had built this for me. He said it was a hideout from my big sister and brother, that no one I didn't tell would know it existed."

A refuge with a crystal ceiling to let in the sun, Darby mused.

"But really, it wasn't their fault," Jonah went on. "It was me always tryin' to keep up with my sister and brother and their friends, then runnin' out of breath. So he built me a spot I wouldn't want to leave."

A kingdom of horses outside and a realm of books inside. What a great father to give an asthmatic boy such a magical place to spend the days he could barely breathe. How many people had such good fortune?

Me, for one, Darby thought thankfully. 'Iolani Ranch was like something from a fairy tale and her grandfather was sharing it with her.

Darby had a hard time reconciling the Jonah who'd flung himself off a running horse into a tangle of wire to rescue Hoku, with the frail boy he'd been, until she saw the wooden horse.

"I love it." Darby pointed to a wooden horse with a huge book set on its back. The horse wasn't painted—just buffed to the brilliant bay of a real horse. "A rocking horse without rockers," she said.

"My dad pried 'em off after I rode hard enough to make me wheeze. After that, I sat on it to read. Until I got tired of my asthma." Jonah gave Darby a half smile. They both knew it was impossible to wish away the chest-gripping disease.

"Now," Jonah said. "It's time for you to pick your punishment."

Outstanding, Darby thought. If her grandfather

was going to let her select her own punishment, she'd pick *none*.

"I don't really need a punishment. I've learned my lesson. I won't ever let Hoku escape again." Darby hoped there was a serious and sincere expression on her face, because she meant what she'd said.

When Jonah's only reply was to raise his black eyebrows, she added, "I know that I hurt Megan's feelings, though, and that none of you really trust my judgment as much as you did before."

Jonah made a rolling movement with his hand as if he expected her to go on.

Darby pulled her knees up against her chest, encircled them with her arms, and pressed her forehead to her knees to concentrate. She didn't know what her grandfather wanted from her.

"Did Ellen—"

Darby looked up at the sound of her mother's name.

"—ever tell you about Mary's bracelet box?"

Darby shook her head. Could Jonah be talking about another relative she'd never met? Or was he about to launch into another one of his random stories?

"Two women were the best of friends," Jonah began, "and when one took sick and was about to cross over—"

"Die?" Darby asked.

Jonah nodded, then continued, "She begged her

friend to become *hanai* mother to her daughter Mary. 'Raise her as your own,' said the dying woman. 'All I ask is that you give her my koa wood box, unopened, when she is grown.'

"Of course the good friend agreed, but she'd always admired her best friend's koa wood box, carved with wondrous birds and beasts and kept on a high shelf. So, after the woman's funeral, she couldn't help but look inside. A polished cinnabar bracelet lay in the box. No great treasure, the *hanai* mother thought, looking guiltily at Mary, but too nice to leave in the dark box until the little girl was grown. So, the *hanai* mother wore the bracelet, growing proud of her slender wrist encircled by the scarlet bangle. She meant to give the gift to Mary someday, but somehow she never did. Her guilt grew each time she took the bracelet from its koa box. Finally, though, she couldn't part with the bracelet. She threw the box into her cooking fire, to destroy the evidence of her theft.

"The flames weren't hot enough to consume her guilt in betraying her dead friend, and guilt poisoned her love for her *hanai* daughter. Mary grew up wild, willful, and, as soon as she could, she moved far away from her *hanai* mother."

When Jonah paused, Darby tried to grasp the story's meaning. She hadn't stolen anything, but she had found something someone had lost. Could he possibly know about the horsehair braids wrapped and tied around her wrist?

Darby's index finger slid inside her shirt sleeve to touch the improvised bracelet, then jerked back. Sharp as a thorn, the broken shell that looked like it had once dangled at the wearer's throat pricked her finger.

Darby curled her fingers tight, in case the shell had drawn blood, but Jonah didn't seem to notice.

"Finally, the *hanai* mother, longing for Mary and forgiveness, knew what she had to do. She sold her house, bought a piece of koa unmatched by any wood in the world, and apprenticed herself to a wood-carver. At first he judged her a ridiculous old woman, but he was willing to take her money. The *hanai* mother turned out to have a talent for the art and the wood-carver was at a loss to understand why the woman created a single box into which she put an old red bracelet, chipped and scratched.

"It took two years, but finally, on bloody feet and with a careworn heart, the *hanai* mother arrived at Mary's door in a strange city. With bent head, the *hanai* mother offered Mary the box and her confession. Crying, Mary drew her *hanai* mother inside and nursed her tenderly until she died."

"I kind of like the story," Darby said, "but I still don't know what you want me to do."

"Every animal on this place earns its keep, but you're a human. You have to earn respect as well as your food and shelter."

Darby stared at the wall until the books blurred before her eyes.

Seeing her confusion, Jonah hinted, "To earn back Megan's respect, you have to understand what you took from her. Then you'll know how to pay her back."

"I hurt Megan's feelings . . . ," Darby began.

"Good." Jonah's voice sounded warm and understanding, like a storybook grandfather. "And how did you do that?"

Feeling ashamed, Darby swallowed, then said, "I made *her* look incompetent." Trying to get this over with, she added, "And I made *you* worry."

"More than that, you took my peace of mind. Ellen told me you were not so brave." Jonah sounded sorry for believing Darby's mother. "But it turns out you're a daredevil when it comes to your horse."

Darby tried to fit his teasing tone with his glare, but then she gave up and just blurted the truth.

"I'm not a daredevil. I just did what I knew was right." Darby shook her head. That sounded lame, like she was quoting something from a leadership class they made you take at school. "*You* know that *I* know how Hoku thinks. Not all of the time, but pretty often. So I knew what was right for her and I had to do it. You do the same thing with horses, right?"

Darby didn't hear how tangled her words were until Jonah bowed his head and gripped the graying hair at his temples with his hands.

Then he boomed out her full name, "Darby Leilani Kealoha Carter, you are wasting time. That, or I'm too old to follow the wandering of a young girl's mind.

"Since you have no ideas for punishment, I'm giving you two chores that will teach you what you need to learn. You're not lacking intelligence, but you're not patient or sensible."

I am too patient and sensible, Darby wanted to protest, *except when it comes to horses,* but Jonah pointed at her as if he were about to make a major pronouncement.

"You will take over tending that goat Francie. Megan's been in charge of her, but now it's your responsibility to see that Francie is fit to eat on the Fourth of July."

Darby winced. She didn't like the idea of eating something that had a name, but she said, "Okay."

"And you'll take over a chore for me. You can serve as Luna's attendant."

"His attendant?" Darby asked. "Like hold his train while he walks to his throne?"

She was joking, but the mighty bay stallion was named Luna, which meant *boss.* And he took his title seriously.

"I'm not sure Luna likes me," Darby said.

"He scares you. That's not the same thing." Jonah held up his palm to keep her quiet. "Luna is a well-mannered, working stallion. He doesn't spook easy, but he will take a stand if you don't. Learning to handle him will be good training for you."

Gooseflesh covered Darby's arms and she shivered, thinking of the proud stallion. "He won't try to fight other stallions, will he?"

"He would if he were challenged," Jonah said, "but he's the only stallion on the place."

"Good," Darby said, then added, "Thanks for giving me such a good punishment. I expected something worse," she admitted.

Jonah nodded and said, "I'm taking it easy on you because you're still learning how things work here."

"Thank you," Darby said. "I think—"

"Don't thank me, and don't think," Jonah told her.

"Don't *think*?"

"That's right. You're too new to this life to think for yourself. I learned that the hard way." Jonah waited for her to contradict him.

He's treating me like a kindergartner, Darby thought, but she stayed quiet.

"Have you cleaned the tack shed?" Jonah asked.

"No. Was I supposed to?"

"You were in there this morning. You noticed that one of the horses had come in and messed things up, yeah?"

"Sure," Darby said, and she knew which horse it had been, too. Kona, Jonah's dappled gray, took every opportunity to sneak into the tack shed for a little of the grain that was also stored inside.

"Who did you think would clean it up?"

Kimo or Cade, Darby admitted to herself, but she didn't say it.

"I'm not sure what I should do," Darby said.

"Make sure the saddles and bridles are hung up. See that the halters are all on hooks, not dropped on the floor. Get rid of the empty feed sacks, and then sweep the floor until there's not a crumb left. I suppose your mother taught you how to use a broom?" He raised one black eyebrow.

"Sure she did," Darby agreed.

"Get after it before dinner," Jonah told her, then scooted to one side to open the door for her.

"I will."

Darby got back down on all fours to leave through the low door. She ducked her head, thinking that once you got to be a year old or something, you really didn't spend much time crawling.

She couldn't shake the feeling that she was leaving a magical place for the ordinary world.

She looked back over her shoulder. Instead of saying good-bye, she said, "I really love your library."

She'd almost made it through the door when Jonah said, "Don't forget. Tomorrow you'll take over Francie."

"The goat," she said.

"Fourth of July dinner," he corrected her.

She sighed, crawled the rest of the way through, then pulled herself to her feet.

Jonah had nearly closed the door when he added, "About the books, help yourself. Anytime."

Chapter 3

Darby opened her eyes and blinked into the darkness.

She heard hooves, lots of them, like an entire herd of horses, moving closer and closer.

She sat up in bed, then sagged against the window frame. She managed to raise her eyelids long enough to look out her window and see darkness. Though the restless hooves moved on, sounding as if they'd passed by the house, there were no horses out there.

Darby flopped back down in her bed and pulled the covers up to her chin. It must have been something like a branch rubbing against another branch, she thought groggily. Invisible night horses didn't exist.

Darby had just found a comfortable position and

drifted back to sleep when it happened again.

She sat up in bed. What had wakened her? This time it wasn't a ghost stampede.

At home, she would have recognized most sounds before she was fully awake. A car alarm might have roused her, or a late bus shifting gears, maybe a lovelorn cat. But she wasn't at home and Sun House sat silent except for the squeak of her bedsprings and the soft rustle of sheets over her pajamas.

Darby leaned forward to listen.

When the sound came again, she recognized the click-thump of a back hoof grazing a carefully placed front hoof. Then—*thud!*—weight bumped against the house wall.

Darby scrambled to her knees and spun around to stare outside. She expected to look down on a rumpled mane, or wide nostrils tilted up at her, but night blacked out everything. Her forehead pressed against the glass, she saw only a moon, thin as the edge of a dime.

But she'd heard a horse. And this time it was no dream.

'Iolani Ranch saddle horses weren't locked up at night, but most stayed in the lower pastures, grazing.

Had Hoku escaped again? No, everyone on the ranch was as determined as she was to keep the filly safe.

Navigator, then? The big brown gelding had kept her company while she cleaned out the tack room yesterday before dinner. Darby guessed it was possible he'd returned and somehow recognized her window.

Wide awake now, she eased her legs from the bed.

Since Jonah slept right down the hall and Darby didn't want to wake him, she rocked from bare heels to bare toes as she headed for the door. She'd read that such a gait was actually quieter than tiptoeing.

Slipping out into a city night would have been risky, but on Wild Horse Island, she had nothing to fear.

A rug slid underneath her on the polished wooden floor and Darby steadied herself against the wall, just as hooves thudded again.

There was a light switch within inches of her hand, but she didn't click on the front porch light. If she were a horse exploring the night, a sudden blast of brightness would scare her away.

But she had to open the door.

She turned the doorknob slowly, hoping the *snick* of metal drawing out of the doorframe wouldn't spook the horse. Then Darby slipped through the barely opened front door.

A dark shape froze as her eyes found it.

The creature couldn't know she was still waiting for her vision to adapt to the night. Darby scanned the shade under the candlenut tree. That's where there'd been motion, then stillness.

A breeze stirred the leaves.

There! Starlight showed her a swath of gleaming blackness. The sheen was too far above the ground to be a panther slipping through the shadows, and too low for an ebony owl spying out dinner from a branch.

Standing stiff so that no sound—not even her arms brushing her sides—came from her, Darby listened.

If she could tell that something was hiding nearby, why weren't the dogs barking?

Canines could see and hear better than people could, and their sense of smell was about a hundred times more powerful than humans'.

Stop holding your breath, Darby told herself, then exhaled in tiny increments.

Maybe she hadn't heard hoofbeats, but heartbeats.

Maybe nothing was wrong, except that her mind had knit a disturbing dream out of leftover worry.

That was probably it, Darby told herself. Her punishment had turned out to be not so bad and her mind was still dealing with its relief.

Maybe.

Determined to find out if her imagination was running amok, Darby took a large step off the porch.

The horse exploded from cover.

Darby heard hide scrape tree bark. She smelled soil and leaves dug up by hooves. A whirlwind snatched Darby's hair and waved the ends against her cheeks.

She heard it. She felt it. She even smelled hot horseflesh. But she didn't see a thing.

The dogs didn't bark. Hoku didn't neigh. And now she was alone.

The kicked-up dust made her sneeze. As she rubbed at her nose, Darby tried to be her usual analytical self.

"Okay, let's look at the possible explanations," she said out loud. Her voice was higher pitched than usual.

She sat down on the front step and laced her fingers together. Looking at them, she told herself to think, but her pulse was still pounding as her mind replayed what had happened.

Darby heard boots as the door opened wider behind her.

Dressed in khaki pants and a pressed shirt, Jonah stood in the doorway.

"It's five o'clock, time to be up," he said.

Darby nodded. Her teeth almost chattered in her eagerness to tell her grandfather what had happened, but she wasn't sure how to explain.

Staring over the ranch yard, Jonah asked, "They bothering you?"

"Who?" Darby knew her grandfather's teasing tone. This wasn't it.

"The *menehune*."

"No, it wasn't little people," she said. Sometimes he sounded serious about weird stuff, and he'd told her before about the *menehune*, who could help or hurt you. "I heard a horse."

"Yeah?" Jonah stepped off the porch. Hands on hips, he surveyed his surroundings. "When?"

"Just a few minutes ago." Darby shifted uneasily on the step. If he asked her to describe the horse, she was sunk.

"Which horse?" Jonah asked.

"I didn't exactly see it. More like, I woke up when I heard hooves moving around. And when I came out here, the horse wasn't gone, but it wasn't really here, either." Darby shook her head. "What I mean is, I could barely make it out under the tree. It held so still"—Darby's hands moved to make a frame in the air—"it just blended in. Then, when I stepped off the porch, it bolted. And I couldn't see what color it was because there was no real light."

Out of breath, Darby waited for Jonah to respond to what might have been the longest string of words she'd put together since she'd arrived.

"Could have been a dream. A night *mare*, you know?" he joked.

"I thought of that," Darby said. "But it smelled like a horse."

"Maybe a spirit horse, then. There's the Shining Stallion of Mauna Kea—a mountain over on the Big Island. He's been stealing mares and breaking down fences for a couple hundred years."

"I don't think—"

"He's sighted at daybreak and nightfall." Jonah gestured at the uncertain light around them.

"Here?" Darby cut in.

"Moku Lio Hihiu?" Jonah gave a skeptical shrug as he pronounced the Hawaiian words for *Wild Horse Island*. "He's been spotted on Sky Mountain and near Two Sisters. There's even a waterfall named for him down in Crimson Vale. But me? I always thought those were stories to scare off people from places that the paniolo don't want to share."

"How would that work? People would be drawn to a story like that, not kept away, wouldn't they? I mean, 'the shining stallion' sounds pretty cool."

"He's a menace, this horse. A killer."

A throwback to a vicious ancestor? Darby wondered, thinking of what she'd heard about her own filly's great-grandsire.

"Oh." Darby considered Jonah's explanation for a few seconds. "But is he really real?"

"People believe what they want to believe, but *I've* never seen him," Jonah said.

Me either, Darby thought, but that didn't mean there hadn't been something breathing under that tree.

She studied the tree for a minute. Its leaves looked like maple leaves, though Auntie Cathy had told her it was called a candlenut tree. Supposedly its pods could be set aflame and they'd burn like candles. Too bad they hadn't spontaneously combusted and given her light to see the horse.

Jonah must have noticed her lopsided smile.

"I'm not pranking you, Granddaughter, just telling you what people say."

Darby sighed. "He's probably just a tall tale, then, right?" Darby gave Jonah her most scholarly look. "Or a ghost-stories-around-the-campfire legend?"

"Something like that," Jonah said. "Because I've only seen two horses with murder in their eyes."

Darby didn't like the sound of that. She loved horses with all her heart, but they were big muscular animals with flashing teeth and heavy hooves.

"But if it was a real horse—maybe a wild horse," she said, thinking of the black horse she'd seen in Crimson Vale, "he'd only come onto a ranch with people around if there was something wrong. Right? Or if"—Darby's breath caught, thinking of Hoku— "he was here to steal mares?"

"Can you see Luna allowing that?" Jonah asked, but for an instant, he looked troubled. Before Darby could ask why, Jonah asked, "Do you know how to make coffee?"

She wondered if she'd ever get used to the way her grandfather's mind hopped around like a Ping-Pong ball.

"Kind of," Darby said, even though her mother always set up a coffeemaker and all Darby had to do was flip a switch. She was tired of admitting she didn't know anything. Besides, she'd figure it out.

Dumber people had learned to make coffee, right?

"You do that while I go let the dogs out," Jonah instructed. "If there's a strange horse around, they'll find 'im. Then we need to talk."

Darby changed into jeans, boots, and a long-sleeved yellow shirt. She buttoned the cuffs. If it got too hot, she could roll them up above her good-luck charm. But only if she was alone.

She kept calling it her good-luck charm, but she didn't know what it was or how she'd ended up with it yesterday.

Auntie Cathy had told Darby that something in her room smelled "musty."

Feeling a little insulted, Darby had gone to her room and, hands on her hips, taken a deep breath. Instantly her nose had wrinkled. She'd smelled what Auntie Cathy had been talking about and *musty* was too nice a word for it.

Darby had sniffed. She'd patrolled the perimeter of her room. Finally, she'd looked under her bed.

Disgusted, she'd retrieved the mildewed jeans she'd accidentally kicked under there after she'd come in exhausted from battling riptides, then hiking home with Hoku.

Darby had picked the jeans up with the thumb and forefinger of one hand and covered her nose and mouth with the other. Then something had fallen on her bedroom floor.

This.

The toothpick-thin braids were bound at each end with stringy stuff she recognized as coconut fiber. There wasn't much left of its centerpiece shell. And that was probably her fault.

Darby thought she'd tripped on the necklace, mistaking it for a vine, as she'd made her way down to Hoku in the cove below the pali.

Darby touched the pale nub of shell. Sharp and cracked off at an angle, it must have snagged on her jeans and stayed with her as she rescued Hoku.

She smoothed the pad of her thumb over the braids. They were smooth and black.

How cool would it be if the hair had come from the shining stallion Jonah had told her about? And what if it wasn't a good-luck charm, but a talisman or amulet? She could never remember which one of those was worn as protection. But if this one had horsehair from the land and shell from the sea, maybe . . .

Stop, Darby ordered herself. It was an interesting souvenir of how brave she and Hoku could be together. Daydreaming about anything more could wait.

Back in the kitchen, Darby checked the cabinets and shelves for a coffeemaker and couldn't find one, but she did find coffee beans. Shaking the airtight jar, she saw that they were hard, oily beans. Dark brown and the size of her little fingernail, they were totally different from the ground-up, powdery stuff her mother used.

They smelled great, she thought, opening the jar, but she wished they'd come with instructions. Why hadn't she watched as Auntie Cathy and Jonah made coffee? Her only idea for making coffee was soaking the beans in water, like tea in a bag. But that seemed wrong.

Well, all coffee required hot water, so she put water in a pan, set it on a stove burner, and switched it on to boil.

While she tried to figure out what came next, she munched on a handful of the granola Auntie Cathy ate every morning. It could be sweeter, but the dried fruit bits weren't bad.

A glance at the kitchen clock gave her an idea. She could call her mother for help.

"Honey, I'm so glad to hear from you!" her mother rejoiced. "You are definitely coming with me when I come back to Tahiti! It is amazing. I'd forgotten—being bred in the tropics . . ."

While her mother rattled on excitedly about Tahiti, Darby poured granola into a bowl and began picking out pieces of dried fruit.

". . . just feeling at home, here. Your grandfather notwithstanding, I bet you're feeling the same."

Feeling at home? Darby drew a deep breath. She hoped her mother wouldn't zero in on her hesitation. Sometimes it was like she could read minds.

"I love the ranch," Darby insisted, "and Hoku is

the best thing that's ever happened to me."

"I'm so happy things are working out," her mother said in a marveling tone.

"I've got to ask you, though—" Darby tried to stop herself because the question on the tip of her tongue wasn't about making coffee. "Mom, did Jonah used to make you pick your own punishment?"

"Darby, what did you *do*?" Her mother sounded horrified. "He only does that for big things. Like, once I—never mind. What did *you* do?"

Darby wondered why she hadn't realized that by tattling on Jonah, she'd be telling on herself.

She stared into the pan full of water. Little bubbles clustered together, then broke away from each other, racing for the surface.

"He didn't tell you about Mary's bracelet box, did he? Darby?"

"Um, was it sort of about an orphan and making amends?" Darby stalled, trying to sound confused. "I'm not positive I understood."

"What I think is that I won't be led off on a tangent, young lady. Now, tell me what you did."

The use of *young lady* was always a bad sign.

"I'll tell you later," Darby said. Watching the water simmer, she realized something for the first time: Jonah hadn't called her mother when she'd been missing.

"Tell me now," her mother insisted. "I'm due on the set in five minutes."

Wisps of steam rose off the quaking surface of the water.

"I accidentally let Hoku get away—"

"You—" Her mother gasped.

"So, I went after her by myself—"

"But you left a note," her mother said. "Right?"

Darby knew she wasn't giving her mother a very accurate picture of what had happened, but she just answered the question. "No, I didn't."

There was a moment of stunned silence before her mother asked, "You weren't gone overnight, were you?"

"No!" Darby insisted.

Was her mother wishing she was close enough to shake her? Maybe she was simply amazed that Darby had done something that required her to put down her book.

"And you're fine?"

"Sure, I didn't get hurt." *Much*, Darby thought, wincing as she touched her bruised face.

"Jonah must have been worried."

"I'm afraid everyone was," Darby admitted.

"Well then, you might as well go along with the punishment. What's it going to be?"

"Taking care of . . ." Darby hesitated. The word *stallion* might worry her mother, so she said, "Some horses, and helping out Megan. She's the ranch manager's daughter and I was supposed to be staying with her until I learned my way around better."

"The buddy system," Mom said approvingly. "That's always a good idea. You know that."

"I do," Darby said, and suddenly she heard rapid steps coming across the ranch yard. She couldn't have said why, but she felt guilty and eager not to be caught talking on the phone. "I better go, Mom."

"Me too—but, Darby? Behave, will you, honey? I've never had trouble with you acting up. Don't start misbehaving now."

"I won't, Mom."

"That's my girl! Hug Hoku for me!" Then, with a smacking kiss, her mother hung up.

Darby pinched a toasted almond out of the granola. Just as she popped it into her mouth, two things happened.

Jonah walked into the kitchen as the coffee water boiled over. Hissing on the hot burner, it sent up a cloud of steam.

Jonah bumped Darby's hand out of the way and grabbed the pan's handle. After he'd moved it, he shook his scalded fingers.

Without looking at her, he muttered, "Go ahead and eat your breakfast, but while you do, I think you'd better tell me more about this horse in the night."

"I really didn't see him that well," Darby told Jonah.

"And yet you think he's a male. A stallion?" Jonah asked.

"Probably just because you told me about the

Shining Stallion of—"

"Mauna Kea," Jonah supplied.

"Why do you want to know?" Darby asked.

"Just tell me what you can remember," Jonah said. He didn't answer her question and suddenly she saw Jonah differently.

He looked totally Hawaiian—powerful and insightful, with his head thrown back like one of his fine horses. She could almost imagine him wearing the feathered helmets of old Hawaiian royalty.

"Is something wrong?" Darby asked.

"Close your eyes and take your time," he coached her.

Then, breaking the spell, her grandfather turned away to sponge up the spilled water with maddening slowness.

Patiently, he pulverized the coffee beans in an electric grinder.

She would never be able to wait him out, Darby thought, so she closed her eyes. Trying not to look like a fake psychic, she made her mind call up a vivid memory of the dark horse.

"He smelled like he'd been running," Darby said, "and when he went past, I felt a wave of warmth." Darby opened one eye. When Jonah motioned her to keep talking, she tried to remember more. "He was almost totally silent. That's why I thought he might be wild—because he'd been stalked before, and managed to escape. His coat must have been black or bay. When the moonlight hit him, he was shiny, but not bright. Not spotted, either, like a pinto or Appaloosa."

Size? Darby didn't know if the word came from Jonah or from her mind, nudging her to see the strange horse again, because, for some reason, it was important.

"He had lots of mane and tail, but he wasn't big. Not much taller than Hoku, but deep-chested. Strong looking."

"When he passed you, where was he headed? Back to some other ranch—toward the Zinks' place, maybe—or on his way to Crimson Vale?"

Darby opened her eyes to see Jonah gesture toward the road.

"He went the other way." Darby pointed toward the tack shed, the fox pens, and Hoku. "So you don't think it was just one of our ranch horses wandering around. . . ."

Jonah's smile erased all traces of his commanding look, but she couldn't have said why until he agreed, "Not one of *our* ranch horses?"

Darby ducked her head. Jonah's expression said he liked her feeling possessive of the ranch and its horses. His approval felt impossibly good.

But the dark horse. She had to know more about him.

"Do you know who he is?" she asked.

"I might know *what* he is," Jonah said, and just when Darby thought he was about to offer another supernatural explanation, he finished, "Bad news."

 Chapter 4

Confident she'd done a good job cleaning the tack shed the day before, Darby thought it would be only minutes before she could mount Navigator and begin the new job Jonah had set for her: finding the strange horse.

"No one saw him, but you got a feel for him," Jonah said. "Now, go down and tell Kit you're there to finish what you started." Jonah moved his coffee cup in a gesture like he was making a toast. "He'll know what you're talking about."

Darby rushed out of the house and across the ranch yard so fast, she nearly collided with Kit in the tack room doorway.

"What's this, now?" the foreman asked.

"I came to finish what I started," Darby explained.

Kit looked up long enough to meet Darby's eyes. For him, that amounted to a stare.

"You in trouble?" Kit asked.

"I don't think so," Darby said.

"Hmm." Kit touched one thumb to his turquoise rock necklace and looked across the yard at Jonah.

Her grandfather stood under the candlenut tree, looking down, walking slowly.

Something was going on that Kit seemed to want to be part of, but he turned back to Darby with a resigned sigh and jerked his thumb inside the tack room.

"It's about these old grain bags," he said.

Darby blinked as her eyes adjusted to the dim light, but she had no trouble recalling three gunnysacks that had once held the horses' grain. She'd seen them tossed in a corner. "I stuffed them in that bucket," she said, pointing. "Just to get them out of the way so I could sweep."

How boring was this compared to tracking down a wild horse? But Darby knew Jonah wouldn't let her leave before she finished up, so she rushed on, "Where was I supposed to put them?"

Kit pulled out one of the bags. As he did, something scattered on the board floor.

"Pieces of grain get stuck in the corners and left behind even when the bags look empty. Old grain gets damp, spoils, and ferments," Kit explained.

Darby's mind raced ahead. "And it draws mice?"

"Not if one of the horses gets in here first," Kit said.

Like Kona, Darby thought.

"That's what Jonah wanted you to know," Kit said. He seemed to be edging out of the tack room.

"But, I locked the door when I left last night," Darby said.

"Yeah," Kit agreed, rubbing the back of his neck.

He seemed uncomfortable, but she didn't understand why. She'd sweep it up and be on her way. But then Navigator's big form blocked the sun falling into the tack room and Darby heard him snuffle.

Did he smell the spoiled grain? *Fermented,* Kit had said. Her mind flashed a nightmarish image of Navigator lying on his side, his belly distended from food poisoning.

"No, you get out of here," she told him, and windmilled her arms at the gelding. "Go on, get!"

Eyes rolling, Navigator backed away from the door.

"Jonah told me to always lock the door and I did," Darby insisted.

"I know." Kit frowned across the ranch yard at Jonah again. "But the boss wants the job finished up."

"I can do that," she said.

The job shouldn't be too dusty since she'd swept

last night, but she wished she'd put her asthma inhaler in her pocket when she'd changed out of her pajamas.

Darby carried the gunnysacks to a wheelbarrow, raked up bits of icky, soft grain, and even used her fingers to pick up a few last pieces. Some were coated in fuzzy mold. She couldn't stand the thought of the horses eating them.

When she could see no more grain, she stood up, scrubbed her hands against her jeans, and ignored her wheezing. She didn't want to go back to the house. She wanted to go ride.

Following Kit's directions, Darby found the ranch compost pile and raked dirt over the sacks while Navigator watched. Darby tried to exhale completely with each breath.

She looked over her shoulder toward Sun House and saw Kimo.

He rode a fractious blue roan, a cow horse in training. Darby wasn't sure of the roan's real name, but she'd heard him called Buckin' Baxter.

She couldn't believe Kimo rode him while carrying a shovel over his shoulder.

The first time she'd seen Kimo, she'd thought he looked square and sturdy as a stone house. He did, but the cowboy also had a Hawaiian flare that always surprised her.

Today, he'd twisted red flowers around his hat band.

"You need to turn that under, yeah?" Kimo extended the shovel as if she should switch with him. "This works better."

Darby took it, careful not to spook Baxter, then glanced up to say, "Thanks."

"Caught you lookin'," Kimo said. With a smile, he tugged his hat brim lower so she had a better view of the blossoms.

"I—" Darby turned away to hide her red face. She poked the shovel at the gunnysacks.

"Wait 'til we really decide to make fancy," he teased.

"I wasn't . . . ," Darby sputtered. Kimo didn't sound offended, but she tried to explain. "It's just, where I come from"—she forced out the rest of the words—"guys aren't that into flowers."

"Think they make me look sissyish?" Kimo asked.

"No! *I* don't. Besides, anybody who can ride Buckin' Baxter and balance a shovel . . ."

Kimo tilted his hat at a more rakish angle.

Darby closed her mouth before Kimo thought she had a crush on him or something. She really should just stop talking altogether.

"My grandfather?" Kimo said. "He tells us it's to show nature we love her. Me? I do it to make the girls smile." Kimo kept talking over Darby's groan. "Besides, the wind'll come up later and their weight will keep my hat from blowing off."

Kimo's easy explanation of Hawaiian ways made

Darby want to ask him about the hooves she'd heard that morning.

Before he could ride off, Darby blurted, "Did you see any stray horses when you were driving to the ranch this morning?"

"No, but I stopped a little. Brought Cathy fresh fish from her favorite pond in Crimson Vale. Are we missing any?"

"I don't think so," Darby admitted, "but really early, before it was light, I thought I heard a whole bunch of horses outside my window."

"And when you looked out, there was nothing there?" Kimo asked.

"How did you know?"

"Probably heard the tsunami horses," Kimo assured her. "There was a little earthquake last night. That's what I heard on the radio. That always stirs 'em up."

Darby wondered if you had to be born in Hawaii to understand the connections between the real and the imaginary. She never knew where Kimo and Jonah drew the line. In fact, she wasn't at all sure they did.

"Long time ago, some farmers down in Crimson Vale felt the Two Sisters — the volcanoes, you know — trembling, and thought there was about to be an eruption. They guessed a big storm would come after, and since they didn't have time to move their stock up that steep road, they just turned 'em loose. Most got drowned in the tsunami."

"You know"—Darby didn't try to hide her exasperation—"this island has more ghost stories than any place I ever heard of."

"Sure," Kimo said with a shrug. "It's the youngest island in the whole chain. Everyone who ever died is still around."

Baxter jumped back a step, pawed the dirt, and then Kimo turned him with a flourish and rode away.

Darby had almost finished burying the sacks for composting when she heard a clang of metal coming from behind the house.

She saw Megan hanging up a bucket. Darby was about to call out, but then the older girl sprinted for the house.

Megan was dressed for school and, as usual, looked perfect, even though she must have been doing some ranch chores before she left.

Darby missed hanging around with Megan, but it was her own fault. Since she had slipped away from the older girl to rescue Hoku, making a climb Megan thought was too dangerous, their communication was pretty much limited to glares, pressed-together lips, and "Pass the rice, please."

"I'm a little lonesome," Darby confided to Navigator, but that wasn't really it. She was sick of feeling like . . .

"A bungler," she told Navigator, and the brown gelding sighed loudly.

In Pacific Pinnacles, neighbors asked her to babysit, to water plants when they were on vacation, to sign for packages delivered while they were at work. She'd been good at lots of things besides writing papers and taking tests. She could get around the city and she'd amused her mother by telling her about interesting stuff she'd read. Like one night just before she'd left, she told her mother what had killed most prehistoric men—skull fractures—and her mom had wanted to know more.

These days, though, she did everything wrong.

Navigator's warm breath stirred Darby's hair against her neck. She closed her eyes, reached a hand back to touch the gelding's neck, and thought, *maybe not everything*.

Somehow, she'd managed to get herself plopped down in the middle of horse heaven.

Smiling, Darby let Navigator nudge her. The big horse wanted her to do something fun.

"It won't be long," Darby told him.

Hoku neighed longingly from her pen and Darby was wrapped in joyful chills. She had a long way to go before she could earn what had been given to her, but she'd do her best.

So what if she felt lonely along the way? She'd sometimes felt lonely at home, too. Here, she had horses!

"Let me go feed Hoku, good boy," Darby said to Navigator, then lowered her voice to a whisper and added, "Then, we're riding out to solve a mystery."

The gelding lifted his head, and his eyes, circled by rust-colored hair, gazed at nothing Darby could see. A breeze strummed the leaves of the ohia tree and his ears pricked to listen. On her first day at the ranch, Darby had thought Navigator was black. Unless she looked really closely, and took the light patches on his muzzle and around his eyes into consideration, he still did. But Jonah had told Darby that Navigator's papers classified him as brown.

What his Quarter Horse pedigree didn't say was that Navigator was a wise horse. Jonah had named the gelding for warriors who'd navigated by stars, birds, and sharks, across hundreds of miles of ocean to reach Hawaii, because the brown horse never got lost.

Navigator blew through his lips, then trotted toward the tack shed, ready to be saddled and on his way.

As soon as Darby had her horse saddled, Jonah called for her to join him.

"I tracked this horse from your window," Jonah said, pointing.

Darby couldn't make out any single set of hoofprints amid the many stamped all over the place, but she followed Jonah as he led her toward Hoku's corral.

"They disappear onto the grass, here," Jonah said. "I'm thinking he went on to the fold, where he's hidden."

Darby had never really looked much past Hoku's new corral, but she saw the grassland ahead, cresting and falling like a roll of green velvet.

"I want you to ride around looking for his hoof-prints," Jonah said. When he went on, his voice sounded secretive. "And I'd appreciate it if you didn't tell anyone else exactly what you were looking for."

When he walked back the way they'd come, scuffing his boot over hoof marks to erase them, Darby thought, *If I'm going on a top-secret mission, I at least better know what I'm looking for.*

"Even though some of them are smaller than others," she said sheepishly, "I can't tell the horses' hooves apart, not really."

"You'll make these out."

Leading Navigator by his reins, Darby squatted to look where Jonah pointed. She felt like a real cow-girl, studying hoofprints in the dirt, because all at once, she saw a hoof mark with a wavy edge.

"Is something wrong with his hoof?" Darby asked.

"I'll explain later," he said, and when he looked up to see Kit approaching, Jonah kicked dust over that print, too.

"Need any help?" Kit offered. "I used to be a fair hand at tracking. Nowhere near's good as my little brother, though."

Kit flashed a smile at Darby and she returned it because she had met the foreman's brother Jake, but she wasn't thinking about Nevada. She was thinking about her Hawaiian grandfather and wondering why the horse she'd encountered this morning was such a secret.

Darby rode for hours, ignoring the tightness in her chest and the growling in her stomach. Hoof marks were here by the hundreds but she didn't see any like the one Jonah had shown her, and Navigator didn't lead her to the trespassing stallion, either.

When she stared at young horses playing chase far out near the Two Sisters volcanoes, Navigator carried her closer to watch. If she twisted in her saddle, trying to make out black volcanic rock running in straight lines, he veered around trees and up hills, taking her near enough that she decided they had to be manmade boundaries.

Once, Darby thought Navigator was on to a clue.

Luna greeted them with a raspy neigh and Navigator gave a glad whinny. The big bay stallion trotted along his fence, snorting some sort of demand.

"What's he saying?" she asked Navigator, but when the gelding failed to translate, Darby looked all around for an intruder and saw nothing but an interested troupe of mares and foals.

A pinch of guilt reminded Darby that Jonah had put her in charge of Luna, but what was she supposed to do? He roamed in his own open pasture. He had a water trough. The field had good drainage and no mud holes where he could slip, no pieces of metal or wire to cut himself on.

Darby shrugged. She'd better ask for more instructions, because he looked fine to her.

She reined Navigator away from Luna's pasture, and the gelding didn't seem to want to go. When she gave a little kick, though, he gave in and jogged across Pearl Pasture toward an elegantly dappled mare.

"Hey, Lady Wong, how's your pretty Black Cat baby?" Darby called. Talking to the horses helped Darby remember their names. "Blue Ginger and Koko, are you girls keeping the flies off each other?"

She smooched at the roan and the fudge bay with the silver mane as the two mares stood head to tail. Clearly the strange stallion wasn't among the mares and foals, and none of them was missing.

Darby guessed she was being paranoid to think that the stallion had come after Hoku, but she'd seen his hoofprints with her own eyes, just yards from her filly's fence.

A raindrop fell, sat trembling and transparent on the back of the hand holding her saddle horn, and then trickled off as another drop hit her hair and pattering began all around her.

The scattered drops became a shower.

"Home or under cover?" Darby asked Navigator, but there was no question that the gelding was headed toward the forest on the other side of Pearl Pasture.

That's where she'd met up with Jonah when she was bringing Hoku home. And if she were a wild horse, that's where she'd hide.

She thought like a horse, imagining fern fronds tickling her flanks as she backed into the foliage. She'd stand still, letting her body blend in with her surroundings. She'd draw shallow breaths, but flare her nostrils to take in the approach of scent-blind humans.

And if she were a stallion, the side-by-side trees would hide her from Luna. She'd peer past a curtain of vines to spy on the beautiful broodmares.

But she wasn't a horse. She was a rider.

Darby straightened in the saddle, and as she rode Navigator downhill, his strides lengthened.

"Slow down, boy," Darby said, shortening her reins, but he didn't seem to notice.

Looking at the fence ahead, Darby was pretty sure she could manage to climb off Navigator, open and close the gate, then use the fence as a mounting block to get back on him.

Navigator must have felt her decision, because he stepped out of a long walk, into a trot.

"Whoa," she told him, closing her right hand over the reins, too.

She didn't want to jerk at his mouth, but the gelding ignored her and burst into a swinging lope. Was he taking her after the invading stallion? Or was he taking advantage of her hesitation?

Exhilaration mixed with worry as the mares and foals joined the friendly stampede. Blue Ginger and Lady Wong loped alongside them. Black Cat zigzagged around the adult horses to gallop on ahead.

Even if Navigator knows what he's doing, I don't, Darby thought. She tightened the reins as the white wooden fence grew bigger and closer, and Navigator's strides shortened.

I really am learning to ride, Darby thought. Just a few days ago, she and Navigator had stalled out here, because she didn't know how to tell him how to back or turn away from the fence. *I'm getting the hang of it.*

She held her head higher, pressed her shoulders back, and took a breath deep enough to lift her rib cage.

Darby was grinning when, in some involuntary celebration of their own, her heels jarred against Navigator's ribs.

The Quarter Horse broke into a run.

Chapter 5

Gently, Darby pulled with her right hand, then her left, but Navigator paid no attention. In fact, her fingers felt the horse set his mouth more firmly against the bit.

Could such a big horse move on tiptoe? He seemed to be doing just that, head high and ears pricked to a beckoning song only he heard.

The white fence loomed closer and closer. At this speed, she didn't dare do anything wrong. Navigator could fall.

And then he stopped.

The small of Darby's back slammed against the saddle cantle.

Had Navigator been bluffing?

"That's enough," she told him sternly.

The horse always heard through the harshness to affection, but she managed to persuade him to slide parallel to the fence and he finally came close to the gate.

Darby stretched her arm far enough that her fingers grazed the bolt, then gripped and slid it. Yes! She'd opened the lock from the saddle.

Her celebration lasted until Navigator pulled at the bit, lifted his nostrils skyward, then headed away from the gate so she couldn't swing it open and ride through.

Darby backed the brown horse. She nudged him with her heels. She turned his head this way and that, but Navigator never put her in a position that worked.

Gritting her teeth, Darby wanted to abandon the task, but she couldn't. If she left the gate open, the mares and foals could slip through, into the rain forest. They might even wander as far as Crimson Vale. Whether she rode through it or not, the gate had to be bolted closed.

Darby dismounted, swung the gate open, and led Navigator through, before dropping the reins to ground-tie him as she'd seen the cowboys do.

Almost done, she said to herself, sighing, and then bolted the gate.

They'd ride a little way into the rain forest, Darby decided. Not because she wanted to be surprised by the horse that had charged out from under the candlenut tree with the power of a locomotive, but because she wasn't eager to come back and fight with this gate again.

She turned back to Navigator and saw he'd taken a few steps away from her.

Don't let him hear panic in your voice.

"Why didn't I keep a death grip on your reins?" Darby chirped. "I'm a dummy, right, 'Gator?"

If the sugary tone was working on the horse, why had he taken another step in the opposite direction? But she didn't give up.

"Hey, boy," she continued sweetly as the horse took another stride, "if you think you're going to strand me out here, you are out of your equine mind."

Navigator broke into a trot, heading away from her.

Oh, no! Her first instinct was to chase him, but after two steps she stopped. He'd just run away from her.

"Navigator," she called. "Come here, good 'Gator."

He slowed and dropped his head to graze. His flattened ears told her he wouldn't come back.

You can do the walking, his snort said, but finally Navigator let her grab a rein.

"Good boy," she said, giving it a cheerful swing like a jump rope.

What did you call that, when you just held the rope low to the ground and swung it gently back and forth?

Darby hadn't jumped rope since she was in

second grade, but the memory made her smile. And then it gave her an idea. She swung the rein up and over, let it graze the ground, then started up again.

Navigator jerked back, feigning alarm, then sighed. Of course, *he* wasn't head-shy.

But Navigator was tired of her nonsense. He blew another patient breath through his rust-colored lips.

"You're right," Darby said, ashamed. "It's time to go back. If you showed me any clues, I'm too dense to recognize them."

Why had Navigator wandered away from her? Because she'd insulted him by treating him like he was her babysitter?

"I'm sorry," she said, "but could you just come with me over to the fence so that I can use it as a mounting block?"

Navigator braced his legs, refusing to stir one hoof toward the fence.

"Please?" Darby pulled on the reins until she was afraid she'd drag the bit out of his mouth.

The Quarter Horse was strong. He could probably tug a truck out of a ditch.

It's going to take more than an apology to make Navigator forgive me, Darby thought as Jonah's story about Mary's bracelet box wormed its way back into her mind.

"I know how to make amends," Darby said gloomily. "Let me get back on and you won't be sorry. I might regret it." Darby grunted as she lifted her left boot with both hands and got it into the stirrup. "But you'll be happy as a lark."

Darby bounced up and slung her leg all the way over Navigator's back. She swallowed hard and held the reins. She could do this.

"Not only will you get double carrots tonight, but you can jump back over that fence."

The horse had tried to jump with her twice. He must enjoy it.

Navigator's gleaming coffee-brown head swung around to nudge her boot.

"Yep, that's what I said. I don't care what I look like doing it, because no one's watching." She glanced around just to make sure. She saw only horses.

She trotted Navigator back toward the rain forest. When she had what she hoped was a long running start, she turned him to face the fence. She wondered if your heart could make your breastbone rattle.

Darby tapped his sides with her heels.

Navigator moved forward, but his trot was hesitant, questioning.

Are you sure about this? his gait asked.

"Let's go!" she yelled, clapping her boots against him again, and he burst into a powerful lope.

Darby held her breath as the gelding gathered himself.

Navigator's dark head rose, blotting out everything in front of Darby.

Mane brushed her face. His forelegs lifted. She was tilting back, fingers cramped around the reins and saddle horn.

Then Darby and the brown horse were airborne. Grace and excitement changed them into creatures of the sky and for one endless moment, Darby laughed out loud.

Then balance urged her to clutch Navigator's neck in a stranglehold.

Navigator did his part, landing with a mere click of hooves on the other side, as if the jump had been just an extralong stride, but Darby was still clutching Navigator's neck with both arms as he settled, then shook like a wet dog.

"You're pretty pleased with yourself," Darby said. It wasn't a question. She was no expert, but she could feel the horse's exhilaration.

She'd read that jumping was an act in which the rider threw her heart over the obstacle and the horse leaped in pursuit of it.

"Not this time," Darby said, slowly straightening in the saddle. "You threw your heart over, but I was just hoping for self-preservation."

Darby let Navigator trot up the hill toward Sun House. She bounced a lot, but Navigator moved with such rollicking pleasure, she couldn't tell him no.

She knew Jonah wouldn't approve.

Just as Navigator crested the hill, Auntie Cathy

drove down the ranch road with Megan in the pas-
senger's seat of the silver Honda. School must be over
for the day, Darby thought as the car passed her.
Singing along to the radio with the windows open,
the two didn't even notice Darby.

For a second, Darby missed her mother, but then
she grabbed her opportunity. Megan was happy. Her
good mood might make her more willing to accept an
apology.

Still singing, Megan swung out of the car.

Her cherry Coke–colored hair shone, though
wisps were sweat-stuck to her temples. She wore
baggy shorts and a grass-stained jersey. The gym bag
slung over her shoulder was unzipped and bulging
with a black-and-white soccer ball and shin guards.
Despite all that, Megan made her soccer uniform
look like high fashion.

But she wasn't a snob, Darby thought.

She and Megan had been on the brink of friendship when Darby had messed things up. She'd
ditched Megan, leaving her to ride home and explain
Darby's insane, over-the-cliff pursuit of her horse.
Megan had missed a game that day, and her team had
lost without her.

Dangling her cleats by their laces, Megan was
striding toward the house when she noticed
Navigator. And Darby.

Now, Darby thought. *Apologize. Just don't sound like
a wimp.*

Megan was right in front of her, eyebrows raised as she waited for Darby to say something.

Auntie Cathy hurried ahead of her daughter into the house, giving them some privacy. With a shrug, Megan started to follow.

Darby gave Navigator a heel thump that sent him a little too close to the other girl.

He stopped on his own as Darby blurted, "Megan, I know I said it before, but I'm really sorry for what I did the other day."

Megan sighed. "Don't act like it's such a big deal."

"Well, it is," Darby insisted.

"Not to me," Megan said.

Darby's stomach rolled, as if Megan's indifference had truly made her sick.

Could Megan just be pretending she didn't care?

"I could make brownies or chocolate chip cookies for your team, since I was responsible for you not being there and them losing," Darby suggested.

"Yeah. That would be great," Megan said.

"How else can I make it up to you?" Darby asked, but Megan just hitched her soccer bag higher on her shoulder and looked embarrassed. "I'm taking care of Francie the goat, so that you don't have to do it."

"Fine. Whatever. I mean, that will give me a few more minutes to get ready in the morning," Megan said. "But doing stuff for me is so not the point."

Asking what *was* the point would make her sound like an even worse loser, Darby thought. Making amends wasn't as easy as it sounded.

Megan gave up waiting for an intelligent reply and sprinted up the steps to her apartment.

I've messed up again, Darby thought. Her hands shook so much that Navigator's head swung around to see what was wrong. She'd actually forgotten she was still in the saddle.

Megan stopped about three stairs up, at eye level with Darby.

"Things will work out," Megan told her. "Just let it go, okay?"

"Okay." Darby's agreement came out on a relieved sigh. As far as she could tell, Megan just didn't have it in her to be a witch.

Chapter 6

Darby longed to throw her arms around Hoku's warm neck and tell her she was glad they had each other. Just like Darby missed the easy friendship she had at home with Heather, Hoku must be lonely for Judge.

Mrs. Allen had sent the old bay gelding, a veteran cow pony from Deerpath Ranch, along as Hoku's shipboard companion, but Jonah had insisted on separating the two horses so that Hoku would bond quicker with Darby.

"Jonah was right," Darby admitted to Navigator as she rode him toward the tack room where she'd unsaddle and brush him, "but as soon as things settle down, maybe after Hoku and I do our time in the jungle, I'm planning a reunion party for Hoku and Judge."

Darby swung her right boot free of the stirrup and over Navigator's back, but balanced on her left stirrup for a second before taking the long step down to the ground. "You're invited to the party, too, big boy," she told the horse.

With Navigator haltered and tied, Darby shook out her saddle blanket, hung it and her saddle, and wiped her bridle's headstall with a clean cloth. She was about to start brushing the big gelding when she overheard Kit and Kimo talking between the tack shed and the bunkhouse.

Then Cade's voice rose over the others', "I don't do girly gossip. Never have, and I never will."

"Sorry, but I've got to go see what they're talking about," Darby whispered to Navigator. She smooched a kiss his way, then said, "I'll be right back."

As she rounded the corner of the tack room, she saw all three cowboys coming toward her. They were afoot, but Cade led Joker by his neck rope. Cade seemed intent on walking faster than the other two.

When they saw her, Cade kept his eyes fixed just past her shoulder. Kit, for a second, looked trapped, and Kimo began laughing.

When Joker's freckled nose gave Darby a nudge, Cade stopped.

"They're trying to put me up to askin' you about the spirit horse," he said.

"There's no spirit horse. He's totally real."

"Told ya," Kit said, and though it felt good to have the foreman on her side, Darby remembered Jonah kicking dust over the intruder's hoofprints when Kit approached.

"Are you sure he wasn't a dream?" Cade teased. "After all the legends people have been telling you, just the wind in the trees could sound like a horse."

Darby wanted to insist she'd smelled and heard the stallion, but she remembered Jonah saying, *I'd appreciate it if you didn't tell anyone else exactly what you were looking for,* and just shrugged.

"Kit thinks there's another stud horse around here," Kimo told Darby. "But there'd better not be."

He hadn't asked her a question, so Darby stayed quiet.

"First thing this morning, I pulled back the curtain and looked down on Luna like I always do," Kit told Darby. "And like I told these two, he was showin' off, all puffed up and proud."

Darby thought of the black flash under the candlenut tree, then noticed that Cade was watching her with serious eyes.

When she glanced away from the cowboys, Kit seemed to think she was waiting for more of his story. "Broncs have left me with stiff knees for life, or I woulda got a better look at what was goin' on. By the time I hobbled out there, Luna was just standing by his water trough."

"And you didn't see another horse?" she asked.

"No. Saw Jonah sniffing around like a blood-hound, though," Kit said. "Then he asked me to—you know." He gestured toward the empty wheelbarrow.

Sure, she'd made a mistake leaving the empty grain sacks behind when she'd cleaned the tack room, but Darby wondered, just like Kit seemed to be doing, if Jonah had just been keeping them busy while he looked for distinctive hoof marks.

Kit bumped his black hat back from his eyes, waiting for her to say something, but it was Kimo who muttered, "Don't know of any stud horses on this side of the island."

"All I'm sayin' is Luna had his make-my-day atti-tude on," Kit maintained.

"Kit's right. I was down there pretty early," Cade said, but he sounded as if his mind had wandered elsewhere.

"Should I do something now?" Darby asked. "I'm supposed to be kind of tending him."

"That Kanaka Luna. He's always restless," Kimo said, as if she should put the horse out of her mind.

"I can tell when a horse is itchin' for a fight," Cade snapped. "And Luna was—all puffed up and ready to kick the heck outta somebody."

It was weird how silence sprung up around them. Even Joker watched Cade as if he sensed how out of proportion the words had been.

"It *could* be that wild stallion again." Kimo's tone

was as kind as Cade's had been defensive.

"Mustangs come onto the ranch?" Kit asked.

"Years back one did," Kimo said. "The stallion that killed Old Luna—this one's sire."

"Why'd he come in here?" Kit pressed him.

"For the food? For the fight?" Kimo said.

"He left without mares?" Kit asked.

Hoku neighed from her paddock as he said it and Darby guessed her concern showed on her face, because Kit tried to comfort her by saying, "There are lots of horse legends in Nevada, too."

"This one's no legend," Kimo said.

Darby made a quick inspection of Navigator's hooves and pulled the halter from his face before she asked, "How many years ago did it happen?"

"Six?" Kimo glanced at Cade.

"Five," Cade corrected him.

Kimo nodded, then explained, "Cade moved in not long after the wild stud ambushed Old Luna down by the fold."

Horses could live to be thirty or older, Darby knew, and whatever had brought the killer stallion to 'Iolani Ranch in the first place could have drawn him back.

And the "fold" . . . Jonah had mentioned that when he'd tracked the strange horse past Hoku's corral.

Darby was about to ask what the fold was, since she'd only heard it used as a place for sheep, when something more urgent popped into her mind.

"Wait, they fought to the *death*?" Darby had read that stallions' trumpeting and pawing—the make-my-day attitude Kit had mentioned—drove off the weaker stallion so that neither horse would be injured.

"I don't know if you really want to hear about it," Kimo said.

"Warring stallions can be ugly," Kit agreed.

"I'm not too delicate to know about it, if that's what you're thinking," Darby told them. "If I'm going to be living here, don't you think you should tell me?"

She took up a soft brush and skimmed it over Navigator's back, paying special attention to the sweaty patches of hair.

"This black stud—pretty rough lookin', yeah?—showed up and just rushed down on Old Luna," Kimo said. "No play fighting, just backed up and kicked the old guy's hind legs until he went down, and by the time Jonah got the rifle, the wild one, well, he'd already whirled around and gone for Old Luna.

"As he aimed, that black stud charged! Hurled himself in the air! Come jumpin' up like he could catch that bullet in his teeth. Or like he wanted to meet it head-on."

Darby shivered and Kimo nodded in agreement.

"Gives me the chicken skin, thinking of how he ran off at a full gallop. We never saw him again."

"Jonah missed." Cade sounded as if he'd heard the story before, but still couldn't believe it.

"He rode after him, but no one asked what happened after that."

There was a hushed moment before Kimo went on, "Old guy that mows grass at the cemetery, says he's seen the 'ghost of the murdering horse' grazing between grave markers."

As Kimo gave an unsure chuckle, Darby's logic returned.

It had to be the same horse. He'd returned and Jonah knew it was him, because he hadn't killed him. At least that's what Darby hoped, because if a supernatural Shining Stallion was hanging around Hoku's pasture, she wouldn't know what to do.

"And you really don't know what made him come onto the ranch the first time?" Darby asked. She'd walked all the way from Crimson Vale to the ranch, and knew how determined she'd had to be. Why would a wild horse do that?

"Don't worry about your filly," Kimo said. "Jonah's not much on second chances. If it *is* the stud that got away from Jonah, I'm guessing he's done for."

Darby didn't know what to say to that. She sure didn't want Jonah to kill a wild horse, but she didn't want a murderous mustang to kick down Hoku's fence and kidnap her, either.

Navigator still hadn't wandered away to join the

saddle horses in the lower pasture. His expression was patient as he watched Darby.

"Your carrots!" she yelped, then darted into the tack room, grabbed two, and came back to the big brown horse while the cowboys went about their late-afternoon chores.

As Navigator chewed with obvious pleasure, dripping carrot juice and horse spit on Darby's boots, she realized how protective she felt of him, too.

She needed to find out what was driving the wild stallion from his usual territory so that he didn't hurt any of the horses she cared about.

Taking a quick glance around, Darby touched her lips to Navigator's neck and whispered, "Jonah said I couldn't pet you, but he didn't say one word about kissing."

Chapter 7

With Navigator turned out and some time left before dinner, Darby began walking uphill to see Hoku. She wanted to try out the idea Navigator had given her.

She knew there were other things she was supposed to do. Jonah had told her she would be in charge of Luna and Francie, the goat.

Since Jonah was nowhere around, she sprinted to catch up with Kit.

He was matter-of-fact as he told her how to care for Luna.

"First, keep your eyes open for a second stallion. Wild horses I know don't fight over territory and here, there's no shortage of water. But there's a load of mares down there. Them, they *will* scrap over."

Kit said Jonah expected her to clean Luna's pasture, hand-graze him, and "pony" him — Kit said that meant leading the stallion alongside the horse she was riding — for exercise until she felt confident she could ride him.

"Thought you started with him this morning," Kit said. Then, before Darby could make an excuse, he asked, "When do you go back to school?"

"I don't know," Darby told him. "Jonah hasn't told me."

Kit's dark features didn't change expression, but his eyes widened for a second. That was the only sign he gave that he was surprised a bookworm like her wouldn't press Jonah for a date.

Kit had always lived on a ranch, Darby thought, so he wouldn't understand that she was making a total mess of this "simple" country life. How would she survive Lehua High School? She might be smart enough, but what if they had different kinds of classes? She kept trying to read that course catalog Megan had brought her, but every time Darby opened it, she only saw one thing: *Eighth grade was in the high school.*

Were they even allowed to do that? In Pacific Pinnacles, sixth, seventh, and eighth grades were together in a middle school. She'd be going from upperclassman to bottom-feeder. Why hadn't someone — like her mother! — told her that before?

Darby thought about calling her mother and demanding an answer, but that wouldn't make sense. Either her mother hadn't known—the school system might have changed since she'd graduated decades ago—or she'd known but didn't want Darby to worry.

After all, it wasn't like she had a choice.

"Are you cold?" Kit asked. He'd been looking past her, so Darby glanced over her own shoulder to see Auntie Cathy approaching, but then Kit said, "You."

"Me? I'm not cold." Darby loosened the arms around her body, then glanced up at Kit's friendly brown eyes. "Have you ever heard of eighth grade being part of high school?"

Kit rocked back on his bootheels as if shocked.

"Never," he said.

Even if he was just trying to make her feel better, it worked.

Cathy waved as she came toward them.

"After you check on Hoku," Auntie Cathy said, calling to Darby while she was still yards away, "I need you to go up to the house and help Megan. You two are doing dinner."

"Auntie Cathy, can you show me how to take care of Francie?"

"Give her goat chow and water, move her chain every so often, and don't—" Auntie Cathy shook her head. "She's fine. I'll show you in the morning. Right now, I get to teach Kit about wild pigs."

"She gets all *da kine* jobs, the fun ones, yeah?" Kimo asked as he swaggered by, tapping his flowered hat.

"Can you teach me, too? About wild pigs?" Darby asked.

"Dinner," Auntie Cathy reminded her. "But you do need to learn to recognize places where pigs have been rooting. They damage crops and grazing areas and they . . . can be dangerous."

Although he inclined his head no more than an inch toward Auntie Cathy, Kit looked oddly sympathetic. Kimo, headed for his maroon truck, glanced back with a sad expression, too.

Darby might have stopped to wonder about Kit's and Kimo's reactions if Auntie Cathy hadn't begun firing off instructions.

"There's a roast in the oven. Rice is in the steamer. Don't let it burn. Make a salad, set the table, and that's it. Now, we're off to find pigs."

Darby went to feed Hoku and pretended to hurry, because she didn't want Auntie Cathy thinking she was leaving the dinner preparations to Megan. But as soon as the two adults were out of sight, Darby smooched to Hoku.

Although the filly was busy eating, she rolled one eye toward Darby. She knew her human was up to something.

"Just eat your hay, baby," Darby urged Hoku and, with hay in reach and no men in sight, the filly did just that.

Earlier, Darby had left the tangerine-striped lead rope over the fence and she hoped the filly had gotten used to it.

Humming tunelessly as she concentrated on Hoku's reactions, Darby held one end of the lead rope in her right hand and passed the other end behind her back to her left. Then she swung it back and forth, letting the rope bounce against the back of her legs.

Hoku flattened her ears in annoyance, but kept eating. Darby knew she had to launch this experiment before the filly ran out of hay.

Darby stepped away from the fence and began jumping rope.

A squeal burst from the mustang. She flinched back from the fence and bolted for the far side of her pen.

"Not last night, but the night before," Darby recited just loud enough for the horse to hear over the swishing rope and skipping feet. *"Twenty-four monkeys came knockin' at my door . . ."*

Darby felt breathless, not from exertion or asthma, but because Hoku wasn't really scared. Her head tilted to one side as if she wanted to look away, but her ears pointed directly at Darby.

"As they ran in . . ."

Hoku stopped pretending disinterest and fixed Darby with an unblinking stare as she moved back toward her hay.

"I ran out," Darby said, and when she didn't do anything more alarming, Hoku walked closer. Hay, not her human's sanity, was really her number-one priority.

Finally, neck outstretched, the mustang lowered her head.

"And this is what they said to me . . ." Darby let her voice trail off and, because Hoku was still watching her, but lipping up hay and swallowing it at the same time, Darby rewarded her by stopping.

As the rope landed softly in front of her, Darby said, "More later, you good, sweet girl."

Darby coiled the rope in slow, easy movements and arranged it back over the fence the way it had been all day.

For a second, Darby thought she heard the feathered rush of wings overhead, but she was wrong. The owl hadn't landed in the ohia tree since she'd come back from Crimson Vale with Hoku.

"Dinnertime," Darby reminded herself. She backed away from the corral, pretending not to hurry. "Hoku, if I don't see you before morning, tell your owl friend I said hi."

Hoku swished her tail and jerked her chin in Darby's direction.

The filly was sending her home, Darby thought with a smile. And then she found herself laughing. There was more than one way to teach a wild horse not to fear a rope. She'd just proven it.

❈ ❈ ❈

After dinner, Darby saw Megan carry in the clutter of brown grocery bags that had been in the ranch office into the living room.

She caught the flash of scissors as Megan inflicted serious damage on a sack, then tossed it aside with a moan.

Hovering in the hall as if she were headed toward her bedroom, Darby asked, "What are you doing?"

"My book has to be covered," Megan said. "I have a notebook and textbook check."

"Oh," Darby said.

Megan set about cutting again. Her creation looked more like the fold-and-snip snowflakes you made in elementary school than a book cover. At last Megan sailed a vaguely human-shaped wad of paper at Darby.

"Paper dolls. Want 'em?"

Darby tried not to laugh. "When is your book check?"

"Tomorrow."

"I could help," Darby said.

"You don't have to." Megan's overly patient tone hinted she thought Darby was still trying to make amends.

"But I like this kind of stuff," Darby said. "Do you have a ruler?"

Megan did, and she scooted out of the way to let Darby rescue the remaining brown bag.

Darby had marked, cut, and folded, then neatly written the book's title on the cover when Megan disappeared upstairs for a few minutes. She had no clue what was going on, until Megan returned with stickers.

"It was kind of plain," Megan said, adding the stickers as a final touch.

Next, Darby helped Megan organize her notebook, filing vocabulary tests, quizzes, handouts, and notes behind section dividers.

"It looks great," Megan said. "But you've set my teacher up for a big disappointment. He'll expect me to do stuff this well all the time."

It was quiet.

Darby was tempted to fill the silence by showing Megan her good-luck charm. The older girl had been born in Hawaii, so there was a good chance she'd have a clue as to what it was. The more Darby thought about it, the more she thought it might be some kind of surfer's amulet. To bring big waves, maybe?

But before she could show her, Megan stood up and walked toward the kitchen where her mother was finishing the dishes.

"Thanks," Megan said over her shoulder.

At least we're speaking to each other, Darby thought as she walked to her room and flopped down on her bed to make a few notes in her dictionary-diary.

She half listened to Megan and her mother talking in the kitchen, but their voices were blurred.

Darby was surprised when she heard Megan's footsteps coming down the hall.

"Hey." Megan knocked with the back of her knuckles on Darby's open bedroom door. "Mom said I could take you down and introduce you to Francie. It's not completely dark yet."

"Okay, it's not like I have homework to do," Darby said, trying to make it sound like a joke. "Besides, I've never met a goat."

Megan didn't hear her, because she was already rushing out of the house as Darby pulled on her tennis shoes.

Once she was ready, a door opened at the end of the hall and Jonah appeared.

Darby's grandfather had been missing all afternoon, so she hadn't had a chance to tell him she hadn't found the horse with the wavy hoof. He'd probably figured it out for himself. He'd barely spoken at dinner, simply grumbling as he shoveled down his roast and rice while Auntie Cathy talked about pig damage.

"I didn't see any of those hoofprints," Darby said quietly.

"He cut through the fold," Jonah said, and his guess sounded more ominous now that she knew about Old Luna's death. "Did I just hear you're going out to check on the goat?"

Darby nodded and Jonah looked pleased. "You've put in a long day. That's what it takes."

Darby ducked her head, accepting his words like a trophy.

"You'll need this." Jonah handed her a flashlight.

"Thanks," Darby said, and then she hurried after Megan.

Chapter 8

"Francie, here Francie goat," Megan called as she and Darby tramped through the warm twilight across the ranch yard.

Megan had already shown Darby where the barley goat chow was kept and demonstrated how to measure out the kid's breakfast.

"You probably knew that baby goats were called kids," Megan said as they came around the back of the house.

"Yes," Darby said. She heard the jingle of a chain being pulled across the grass just as Megan held out her hand for Darby's flashlight.

She turned it over and Megan spotlighted a small black-and-white goat, not much bigger than the dogs.

Soft ears flopped at the sides of Francie's head, then waved toward the girls.

"Won't something eat her? Staked out like this?" Darby asked.

The goat made a bleating sound, as if protesting Darby's question.

"Shhh," Megan said. "Of course not. Walk up to her slowly until she gets to know you."

"Oh, you are the cutest animal I've ever seen," Darby whispered. She bent to pet the small goat. Francie's black-and-white coat felt silky. In the flashlight's beam, the goat's shiny little lips were thin as a pink pencil line.

She bumped her tiny horns against Darby's hand.

"She wants you to scratch her head," Megan said quietly.

Darby did, feeling more at ease than she had all day.

"We can't let Jonah eat her," Darby told Megan.

With an alarmed *naaa*, Francie bounced unbending front legs at Darby.

"Shh. You need to be quiet with her so she can settle down for the night," Megan put in quickly.

Darby knelt next to Francie and stroked the white curve of her throat. It was one of the softest things she'd ever touched.

"In the morning, she's frisky," Megan said, and Darby could tell she didn't like the idea of the little goat being meat, either. "You can play with her."

"I will! That's cool!" Darby said.

"Just be careful," Megan said. "Francie will eat your shoelaces if she gets a chance."

Megan returned to the house alone while Darby used the flashlight for one more trip down to see Hoku.

Once she finished checking on her filly, Darby's eyes were accustomed to the darkness and she clicked the flashlight off.

The sky was so star-filled, it had turned from black to charcoal gray. Endless and overwhelming, it almost seemed to be lowering.

Soon she'd be able to touch it, Darby fantasized as she meandered back toward Sun House.

A movement caught her eye. Off the bluff, in the pastures down below, something seemed different.

It was probably just a ranch horse, not the Shining Stallion, but Darby flicked on the flashlight.

Darby caught sight of Jonah, still as the stone he leaned against, with a rifle resting over his forearm.

Was her grandfather waiting for the stallion that had killed Old Luna? Was he going to make sure that this time the challenger and not the challenged would die?

Jonah's impatient voice shattered the drama of the moment.

"Turn that off and come down here," he shouted up to her.

Darby swooped the flashlight's beam away.

"Turn it off, I said, or you'll wreck your night vision."

Darby hurried along the gravel road, past Sun House, then turned right. Placing her tennis shoes carefully, she began the descent down to her grandfather.

She was breathing hard from exertion when she reached him. Still, she managed to ask, "Are you going to try to shoot him again?"

Jonah drew a quick breath, then let it out in a grim laugh.

"Kimo been talking story with you?" he asked.

Darby wasn't exactly sure what he meant. "He told me about the horse that killed Old Luna."

It was exciting to have a secret with Jonah, but she hated the idea of a horse dying for no reason—or for some reason they couldn't figure out and fix.

"Sometimes I think I should have killed that horse," Jonah told her.

But he hadn't. Jonah told Darby how he'd ridden into the forest after the horse. There he saw that his shot had creased the stallion's neck, and when the animal finally fell down in the mud it was breathing so hard, blood sprayed out on Jonah's boots.

"I was standing over him with the rifle, ready to do it, when I remembered yelling at Manny—that'd be Cade's stepdad—just a few days before, for shooting wild horses in his taro patch. Figured if Manny was to blame for running the horses off his land and onto mine, then I killed that stallion, I wasn't much better than him. And that's a thought I couldn't tolerate. Still can't.

"So, I gave that horse—" Jonah interrupted himself. "That stud was more shocky than hurt, so I didn't put him out of his misery. Really, it looked like he was going to be okay." Even in the moonlight, Darby could tell her grandfather thought it was wrong to leave an animal suffering.

"Yeah, I gave him a second chance, but I marked his hoof so that if he ever came back, I'd finish what I'd started."

Darby felt chills at the same expression Jonah had used when she'd been told to get rid of the old grain sacks.

"I meant to use my knife to engrave an X deep on the bottom of the hoof wall, but he kicked me, then struggled up. By then I just wanted to get out of his way, so I only left a kind of a wavy line on him."

Darby sighed.

"Do you think that's cruel?" Jonah asked.

Darby wasn't sure. She thought naming and raising a goat for food was awful, but she was no vegetarian. She'd wondered if Auntie Cathy actually hunted the wild pigs that were tearing up the horses' pasture and she knew that while Jonah had been leaning, with a knife in his hand, over the stallion, he could have done something much worse than notch his hoof.

"No, I don't think it was cruel," Darby said, and she meant it.

But she also believed that if the stallion charged out of the darkness to confront Luna, Jonah would make sure that the wild horse didn't come back again.

Darby's dream was lit by firelight.

Aged Hawaiian women sat side by side, rocking in place. They sang mourning words she could not understand. They stared down at something she could not see. Their black gowns merged with the darkness behind them. Orange feather lei encircled their necks.

An old-fashioned brass skeleton key levitated up among them, but they turned their brown, wrinkled faces away from it. Their mouths drooped in profound sadness as they looked into Darby's eyes and reached toward her.

Darby woke with the sad music vibrating through her. It only took a moment to realize it wasn't golden firelight pressing against her eyelids; it was sunshine.

She'd slept later than usual, maybe because it was Saturday. Instead of rattling around in the kitchen with Auntie Cathy, or running her hair dryer upstairs, Megan must be sleeping in, too.

Darby rolled to her back and studied her bedroom ceiling. It spread smooth and white above her, an opposite to the cave in her dream.

I'd rather dream of horses, she thought, but the

dream had been kind of interesting. Did feather leis even exist? She thought all leis were made of flowers, but she'd come straight from the airport to this ranch.

Maybe Jonah had books about Hawaiian history and culture in his library. If she knew more about the island, she might be able to figure out what the dream had meant, Darby thought as she dressed.

No, you wouldn't, she corrected herself. Dreams were just the brain's way of processing hopes and worries.

The morning was already hot and Darby would have put on a tank top, except that would expose her good-luck charm. Still, she didn't want anyone to see it and think she was superstitious, but she really needed to show it to someone who might know what it was. Because, to tell the truth, she was getting sort of unbalanced about it.

Right then, for instance, she had the eerie thought that the old ladies in her dream were reaching out to her, asking her to return the necklace—that's what it had to be, didn't it? Since it wrapped around her wrist three times?—or they'd keep sending the Shining Stallion after it.

Darby shook her head and looked at the braids.

It was a lot more likely the dream sprang from the "Mary's bracelet box" story, instead of the thing's paranormal powers. If so, why couldn't she make herself get rid of it? Why was she pulling on a long-sleeved white T-shirt instead of something sleeveless?

"It's a mystery," Darby muttered to herself, but she didn't change her mind.

Darby darted out onto the lanai before she left the house. From here, she had the best view of 'Iolani Ranch.

Jonah wasn't still standing guard with a gun down by Luna's compound and she saw no equine corpses.

Everything was fine this morning. Sky Mountain presided over the horizon, looking down on acres of green pastures. It reminded Darby of being a little kid, rolling down grassy hills in the park with her dad until they were both dizzy and their sides ached with laughter.

She should call her father and tell him how wonderful the ranch was, Darby thought as she released the dogs from their kennel. She waved at Kit as he rode past.

But he was leaning forward, frowning, as he set his horse out at a far-reaching jog, and Darby wondered if something was wrong down in the pastures, after all.

Darby headed for the goat chow bin in the tack room.

"Morning," Cade greeted as he bent to use a pick on his Appaloosa's hooves. Darby noticed that Cade's loose brown shirt was collarless and buttonless. With just a slash for his head to go through, it looked primitive, but it had pressed lines down both sleeves.

Just like Jonah, Darby thought, then guessed that the last time she'd ironed anything had been in September, for the first day of school.

"Hi," she said, slipping past.

When Cade asked, "How soon do you want to work with Hoku?" Darby pretended she couldn't hear him over the rush of goat chow pouring into Francie's bucket.

She wasn't avoiding Cade. She just didn't want him watching her with Hoku. She was pretty sure jumping rope wasn't a paniolo-approved method of horse training.

"After your chores?" Cade went on as Darby emerged carrying the bucket.

"Okay," Darby said.

Cade nodded.

Ninety percent of Cade seemed like a tough, uncomplicated guy. He wore that paniolo shirt. He yearned to live the paniolo life, taking all the roughest, open-country chores Jonah gave him—and he didn't mind making sacrifices to do it. He clearly loved Joker and the Appaloosa loved him back.

Left to her own conclusions, Darby guessed she would have decided Cade was just the strong, silent type of cowboy. But Megan had warned Darby that she "didn't know what Cade was capable of."

Still, when Cade had been edgy yesterday, Kimo hadn't taken offense.

Maybe, Darby thought as she swung the bucket

to attract the attention of the little goat, it was just that the return of the wild horse had stirred up Cade's bad memories of his stepfather.

Francie made a *naaa* of recognition when she saw Darby.

In the daylight, the goat's markings looked like a melted hot-fudge sundae, Darby thought, smiling.

Megan had told her Francie was frisky in the morning, and she seemed to be, darting to the end of her chain, then bucking, as Darby sprinted her way.

I'm dancing with a goat, Darby thought. *This time last month, who would have guessed!* She laughed and zigzagged. At first Francie mirrored her. Then a bark and the sound of running paws told Darby the dogs were joining in her scatterbrained antics.

The goat ran to the end of her chain, looking frantically for an escape.

"No!" Darby yelled. "Bad dogs!"

They slowed to a walk and hung their heads.

As Darby turned to calm the goat, she realized Francie had suddenly gone quiet.

Francie's legs stiffened like broomsticks. Her head pitched back, staring skyward, and then the little black-and-white goat collapsed.

Chapter 9

$\mathcal{H}$ad Francie had a heart attack? Could goats die so quickly?

Darby's fingers went limp. The feed bucket clanked on the ground.

Still, Francie didn't move. All four of her legs remained rigid.

I killed her, Darby thought.

She glanced around for help. "Cade! Kimo? Come here! Please hurry!"

Cade came running. A truck door slammed, and Kimo hurried toward her, too.

"What?" Cade yelled.

She pointed and Cade hurried past her.

Darby covered her eyes. She didn't want to look,

didn't want to think what Jonah would say. The chain jingled. She imagined Cade lifting the little goat into his arms.

But when she forced herself to look, Cade didn't have his mouth pressed to Francie's shiny little lips giving her CPR.

Instead, he stood with his arms raised out to his sides, as if he'd been about to swoop down on her, but halted.

Francie was standing up! She shook her head, and the fur-covered bobbles on her neck trembled. One hind leg jerked in a testing kick. Her tail twitched and her tawny eyes looked bewildered until she sniffed the breeze. Then she lowered her head, homed in on her scattered breakfast, and began eating.

"She *was* dead," Darby said slowly. "At least, she looked like it."

"Sure she did," Kimo teased.

"It's not funny!" Darby snapped.

"Francie's a fainting goat," Cade explained.

Darby stared at him.

"Did you say 'fainting'?" Darby asked.

Cade nodded.

"About once a week, something scares her, and over she goes," Kimo explained.

"That's why she's out here, where it's pretty quiet," Cade said.

Chained under the lanai of Sun House, Francie

would be sheltered from sun and rain. No trucks would rumble by too close, Darby thought, and no strange horses would be charging down paths to the pastures below.

"The dogs are usually pretty good about leaving her be." Kimo frowned toward the dogs. They'd crept closer after Darby had scolded them, but Kimo's glare sent them slinking off again. "Jonah didn't tell you she was a fainter when he told you how to feed her?"

"It was Megan. I guess she forgot," Darby said. "Does fainting hurt her?"

"Doesn't seem to," Kimo said. "It's a breed trait."

"There's a whole *breed* of fainting goats? An animal that passes out when it's under stress couldn't make it in the wild."

"It's a man-made breed, yeah?" Cade glanced at Kimo.

"My dad says they were bred by shepherds. If wolves came down on a herd, the sheep ran. And the goat, uh, distracted the wolves."

Darby recoiled, then shook her head and said, "Nice deal if you're the sheep."

Later, after Francie had eaten her fill and Cade and Kimo had gone up to the office to talk with Cathy, Darby ran to Hoku.

"It's just us girls," she called quietly, then fed the filly and asked, "Are you ready for another jump rope song?"

While the filly was still distracted by her hay, Darby began jumping and whispering, *"Down in the valley where the green grass grows, there stood Hoku, pretty as a rose. . . ."*

It was working. Just as the filly had loved her stories in the snow, she seemed to like the jump-rope rhymes. *And she's learning I won't hurt her with the rope,* Darby thought, *so I'll be leading her around in no time.*

"She sang, she sang, she sang so sweet, along came . . ." Darby caught her breath, trying to think of horses Hoku would encounter here. *"Uh, Luna, and kissed her on the cheek. How many kisses did Hoku get? One, two, th—"* Darby missed a step.

When she stumbled, Hoku only glanced at her. That was a good sign, Darby thought.

Still carrying the rope, she slipped inside Hoku's corral before someone could caution her not to.

Hoku kept eating until Darby moved the lead rope. Before Darby could drop her arm back to her side, Hoku doubled away, her bright sorrel body curved like a drawn bow.

Darby had just noticed that Hoku's neck didn't look strained or swollen anymore, when a swing of the filly's hindquarters almost knocked her off her feet.

Winded by surprise, Darby gasped. "So, the rope's okay outside the corral, but not inside?"

She crossed the corral and dropped the rope outside, wishing she hadn't rushed things.

"We can wait, girl," she said. By this time next week, she and Hoku were supposed to be living in the jungle, but Darby was in no big hurry for that.

Time was a weird thing, Darby thought as she leaned against the sun-warmed wood of the fence. She angled her face toward the sky.

If someone had asked her on Valentine's Day what she'd be doing in a month, she would have guessed that at this time of day, in March, she'd be in her second-period class or, on a Saturday, swimming with Heather. She couldn't have predicted she'd be warming up in the Hawaiian sunshine while her mother was shooting a movie in Tahiti.

Hair stuck to her sweaty neck. Darby swept her hand up from her nape and tightened her ponytail. Sighing, she closed her eyes and pushed away nagging thoughts of getting down to the lower pasture to fuss over Luna.

The big bay could probably take care of himself, but Jonah spoiled him. Darby took a few more minutes to bask in the sun.

She heard Hoku's hooves, then her breathing, nearby.

Don't open your eyes, Darby cautioned herself, but Hoku startled a laugh from her by tapping her chin on top of Darby's head. Next she rubbed her nose on Darby's bare shoulder.

The filly's whiskers weren't prickly like Navigator's. Was that because they'd never been trimmed? Or because she was only two-and-half years old?

"You're practically a baby," Darby whispered to the filly, and Hoku let her chin grow heavy on Darby's shoulder, then exhaled as if she hadn't relaxed for days.

This is what I've always wanted, Darby thought. She felt suspended in a golden sphere with her golden horse.

Hoku's snort made Darby's eyes open. She saw the taut line of Hoku's neck and knew the filly saw a man.

Darby followed Hoku's gaze.

Jonah rode his big gray gelding past the old fox cages. Thinking of Jonah's pride in her last night, when he'd mentioned she was a hard worker, or something like that, Darby smiled.

But tension charged Hoku's flattened ears and lowered head, so Darby stepped away, opened the gate, and locked it behind her.

Kona came toward them under perfect, collected control, but his eyes rolled and he jerked up each hoof, as if the dirt burned him. The gray gelding was nervous.

When Darby saw the cold set of Jonah's features, she knew why.

"Bad news, Granddaughter," Jonah said, but he looked calm. In fact, he was actually carrying a cup of coffee with his right hand and his reins in his left.

"What's wrong?"

"It's Luna. We need to discuss your care of him."

She'd looked at him yesterday when she'd ridden out on Navigator, but she hadn't seen anything wrong. Darby's mind raced. Luna had been loose in his huge grassy field, so he couldn't be hungry and his pasture couldn't need cleaning that badly.

"I wonder why you didn't tell me about the activation switch on the automatic waterer, so I could fix it?"

"Activation switch?" Darby repeated.

"The part horses nudge to make the water flow. The one in Luna's trough is broken."

Kit had mentioned Luna standing by his trough yesterday. Is that why Kit had looked so worried when he'd gone riding past on Biscuit this morning?

"How would I have noticed?" Digging her fingernails into the board behind her, Darby tried to tough out this encounter, but bravado wasn't her strength and she knew it.

Jonah flung out the dregs of his coffee as if he couldn't discuss this while slaking his own thirst.

"He drank his trough dry."

Darby closed her eyes for an instant, wishing she could escape.

"Is he okay?" she asked.

"Luna? Sure. He took care of himself by jumping the fence into the weanling pen and drank their water."

Darby imagined the big bay shouldering his

motherless offspring aside. To them, he'd look like a monster.

"Are *they* safe?"

"He didn't hurt 'em, but they're dehydrated. Little guys were scared to go for water while he was guarding it."

Darby didn't see how she could make so many mistakes, but she refused to let her dream life turn into a nightmare for the horses of 'Iolani Ranch.

In two weeks, she'd put three horses—Hoku, Navigator, and Luna—in danger. Multiply that by two, Darby corrected herself. Kona and Joker had been ridden very hard, searching for Hoku. And so had Biscuit.

And now the weanlings . . .

"Maybe . . . ," Darby began, biting her bottom lip hard, hoping the sting would distract her from what she needed to say. But it turned out she couldn't bite that hard. "Maybe I don't belong here."

"I was thinking that you loved the place." Jonah raised his black eyebrows.

"I do!"

"You give up awful easy for someone in love." Jonah cleared his throat.

"I don't want to hurt any more horses," Darby protested. "I'm just not catching on fast enough."

"Need any help packing your bags?" Jonah offered.

Then he smiled.

"Why aren't you mad at me? Or are you?" Darby had never felt so confused. "Why do you want me to stay when I've done nothing but mess up since I got here?" she asked him.

"Don't fish, Darby." Jonah gave a disapproving scowl.

"Don't—?"

"You're fishing for compliments. And here's what I have to say about your 'messing up': I know where you went into the water, and I know where you came out. You have what it takes."

Darby almost quit breathing, she was so surprised. No one was supposed to know she had risked her life to save Hoku. She hadn't meant to do anything but swim her to the beach around the point. Since she was a strong swimmer, it hadn't seemed at all heroic. But she hadn't known about the powerful riptide.

Physical bravery? To her, it was a terrible accident that she'd barely survived. If anything, Jonah should admire Hoku for saving his granddaughter's life.

"And I *am* mad." He pointed his finger at her. "Ask Cathy. I was roaring when I came to the house looking for you. If you'd hurt that stallion or his babies . . ." Jonah grappled for control, but his rational approach collapsed and he was shouting again. "When I ask you to do something, it must be done, and not two or three days later, either!

"It's fine that you work Hoku and go riding on

Navigator, but there's never enough time to do what must be done to keep this place running. Never has been and probably never will be. Why do you think—?" Jonah broke off with a dismissive gesture.

Had her grandfather been about to mention her mother? Or maybe her aunt Babe, who'd opened a fancy resort instead of working on 'Iolani Ranch?

Jonah lay the flat of his hand on Kona's neck, calming the nervous horse.

"We take these animals from places where they care for themselves. We make them helpless, in a way, but they do their best to work with us. They shouldn't suffer for their loyalty."

"They shouldn't," Darby echoed. Her throat ached when she thought of Hoku.

Darby's thoughts tangled together. If not for humans, Hoku would be running free on the open range. If that bus hadn't slid on an icy road, Hoku wouldn't have been captured. If there hadn't been a barbed-wire fence in this strange new world . . .

"I'm sorry," Darby said, knowing it wasn't enough.

"You're smart," Jonah told her. "So how's this? I'll show you what to do instead of expecting you to figure it out. Just pay attention. I won't keep repeating myself."

"That would be great," Darby said.

The owl she hadn't seen for days coasted overhead. Darby looked up quickly enough to see its childlike face and lemon-drop eyes before it vanished into the branches of the ohia tree next to Hoku's corral.

Then, hooves danced behind Darby. Looking over her shoulder, Darby saw her horse.

Cautious, with delicate ears flicking forward and back, Hoku hovered near the fence. She was still afraid of Jonah, of all men.

She was ready to run, but willing to stay if she had to.

"You've got my back, right, girl?" Darby whispered.

Hoku didn't utter a sound. But she flung her head high, showing off the star on her chest like it was the badge of a superhero.

Chapter 10

Together, Darby and her grandfather admired Hoku.

The mustang filly was recovering from her sea journey. Rolling on the warm Hawaiian grass had helped her shed the dull hair from her coat. Her hollow face and sunken sides were filling out from hay, and though the gleam in her eyes was wild, Hoku looked less haunted.

"If her Quarter Horse half beats down that wild blood, your filly might turn into a passable horse," Jonah said.

Darby loved her filly's wild side. She didn't want it beaten down, but she'd heard the dare in her grandfather's voice. She kept quiet, without hiding her smile.

"You going to have her ready to lead in a few days?" he asked.

"I think so," Darby said, but she didn't mention the jump rope.

Jonah grunted, then changed the subject without warning. "Hear the goat surprised you."

"Yeah," Darby said.

"Megan feels bad she didn't warn you."

"Is that what she said?" Darby asked, wondering how Megan could have forgotten something like that.

"She didn't have to. I was up at the house when you screamed—"

"I didn't scream," Darby insisted. "I never scream."

"—and she knew exactly what had happened. Even told me to go easy on you about Luna because she felt so bad about forgetting."

Darby was thinking this over when Jonah made another turn in the conversation.

"Once I got a roping horse, Nell, from a friend on Maui. Cheap, too, because she was fussing with a high-dollar Appy mare of his. Biting her, kicking, and you know in the old times, lots of Appaloosas had little rattails. Nell made a special point of plucking mouthfuls of hair from the Appy's tail. After a while, it was nothing but sore, pink skin.

"So I took Nell. She worked for me, but the mare had no spark and she was off her feed. Soon I got a call from my friend asking did I want to return Nell or take the Appy, because much as the two carried on, they were such good friends, the Appy had been deafening them all, calling after Nell ever since she'd left."

Darby sighed.

It wasn't the first time Jonah had used an animal story to point out something about people.

"I get it," she told him. "You think Megan and I should be friends, even though we've gotten off to a rough start."

"Granddaughter, I don't know what you're talking about," Jonah said. "I was only telling you about a couple horses."

Darby let him have it his way, but she couldn't help wondering if he was thinking of her or Megan as the one with the rattail.

True to his word, Jonah explained how and why she'd be leading Luna alongside Navigator.

"It's exercise for Luna and good training for you," Jonah said as Darby rode Navigator beside him, on their way to the stallion's pasture.

"We 'pony' horses—like they do taking racehorses to the post, you know?—for lots of reasons," Jonah said. "Maybe we've got an injured horse that's not moving around enough to get better; we pony him. We could have more horses to work than we have time to work them. Ponying, you double the number of horses you work out at once.

"With a young horse like Hoku who's not saddle broken, pony her and she'll just naturally copy the behavior of a good solid horse like Navigator."

If I can get her used to the rope, Darby thought.

"But Navigator's the key," Jonah told Darby. "Don't you use any horses but him to pony. The lead horse must listen to you, not his instincts. Kona, for instance, is fine to use with grown horses, but he wants to nip some sense into the young ones."

Jonah went on to say Darby would give Luna two thirty-minute sessions a day in the arena. Once she could handle him well there, she was supposed to take him into open country to keep his back and legs built up.

At first, Luna treated her as he had before, when she'd helped Jonah position him for the farrier, as if he saw no reason for Darby to intrude on his time with her grandfather.

The full-maned bay stallion loped out to meet Jonah, even though they'd probably just seen each other when Jonah had taken him out of the weanlings' pasture and put him back in his own. It was a warm greeting, but one of equals. Instead of petting the stallion, or letting him nuzzle his palm, Jonah gave the stallion a firm slap on the neck.

Like a handshake between partners, Darby thought—as if Luna and Jonah shared the ruling of this ranch.

"Go halter him," Jonah told her. "Tell him 'drop' and he'll put his head down for you. Use one-word commands. He doesn't like a lot of chitchat."

Darby nodded.

"Stride out there. Show him you're in charge. He respects authority."

So she did. Luna turned his eyes her way. There was no accusation in them—he didn't know she was the one responsible for his thirst. His gaze was distant, but not unfriendly. He stared past her, toward Jonah, until the breeze shifted.

As if he thought she was hiding a carrot cake behind her back, Luna came toward Darby at a fluid lope. She didn't get a chance to tell the horse "drop." He stopped beside her and lowered his head, but not for the halter.

I'm not ticklish, Darby told herself as she wriggled away from Luna's sniffing of her head and neck. He was so persistent, it was hard not to laugh.

He rubbed his face into the curve where her neck turned into her shoulder, and Darby stumbled.

"Push him away," Jonah told her. "Hard."

She did, and Luna stepped back. As he returned to being his mannerly self, the stallion opened and closed his eyes, looking baffled.

"Never seen him do that. He was acting like a darned cat," Jonah said. "Could be he likes your perfume."

Darby opened her mouth to say she wasn't wearing perfume, then stopped.

Luna's fascination with the top of her head and side of her neck could be explained in one word: Hoku.

The wild filly's scent was the perfume Luna liked.

She haltered the stallion's bowed head as he stood daydreaming, but she whispered a stern message: "She's my horse and she's too young for you, so you can just forget it."

Darby thought she was doing pretty well when Luna walked beside her as if she were parading him in a show ring, but when they came to the fence, she could tell that Jonah's approving nod was for his horse.

"Switch me horses," Jonah said, once she'd led Luna from his pasture.

She wasn't sure what he meant until he swung into Navigator's saddle and indicated she should mount Kona.

With Jonah in the saddle, Navigator was a horse transformed. Jonah didn't readjust her stirrups, just rode with his legs free, and Navigator moved as if his greatest joy in life was reading Jonah's mind.

Jonah gestured for her to give him the stallion's lead rope, and began firing off instructions on how to pony when he noticed Darby was still afoot.

"Mount up," he said.

"I'm not sure I can handle Kona," she said, looking at the muscular gray gelding as he grazed nearby where Jonah had ground-tied him.

"That old weed-eater? Just climb on," Jonah told her. "You'll be fine."

Darby picked up Kona's reins and got one boot in the stirrup, but then she hopped around on her other foot, making backward circles as Kona kept walking toward her. When he finally tired of the game, Darby swung aboard, then realized it had been so easy because Jonah's stirrups were much longer than hers and her legs were flapping loose, too. Holding on tight, she clucked Kona into a trot.

Luna moved alongside Navigator with such grace, the two seemed to have choreographed this routine and danced it together many times.

Darby sighed at the perfect coordination of rider and horses until they passed near Sun House and the candlenut tree.

Luna swung around as if someone had called his name. With nostrils flared, he bared his teeth and lunged to the end of the lead rope. He would have dragged Navigator toward the tree if Jonah hadn't hissed a reprimand.

Luna satisfied himself with—well, to Darby it looked as if the stallion was marking his territory like a male dog—and then he followed Navigator down the ranch road, strutting as he passed the tack shed.

Darby's mind whirled, certain the intruder had been a stallion. Her thoughts didn't go much farther because once they passed the fox cages, Luna scented Hoku.

Already full of himself, Luna tucked his chin to his chest and arched his muscular neck. He pranced toward Hoku's corral as if he were the king of the island.

Jonah motioned Darby to ride up closer. When she was beside him, he didn't comment on Luna's behavior. Instead, he told her, "Using the saddle horn, you can take a dally if you need a little extra control or leverage."

Leverage on the horse, she assumed, but what was that other thing?

"Dally?" she asked.

"Like this." Jonah flipped the lead rope in a tight loop around the saddle horn and reeled Luna a few steps closer to Navigator.

They were even with Hoku's corral now. Darby's heart pounded hard. How would her filly react to Navigator, Kona, and Luna? Would Hoku's herd instinct kick in and send her hurtling against the fence rails as she tried to join them?

Prancing and champing his jaws, Luna attracted Hoku's attention, but Jonah's smile vanished when the filly pinned her ears and rushed the fence with a squeal.

Luna froze in bewilderment.

"Are you watching?" Jonah asked Darby.

"Yeah," Darby said, surprised. "I thought she'd want to come along with us."

"Not that," Jonah said. "This." He nodded to his saddle horn.

Darby watched Jonah take a second dally in slow motion.

Luna tossed his black mane and snorted before letting himself be towed along.

"Could be she's one of those tomboy mares," Jonah muttered, and Darby couldn't tell if he was talking to her or Luna. Before she could ask for an explanation, her grandfather said, "You need gloves, but more important than that, is this."

Jonah grasped the rope with an exaggerated thumbs-up motion. "Don't ever let your thumb get in the rope's path. Even an experienced rider can be surprised, and when a one-ton horse hits the end of that rope wrapped around your soft little thumb, it'll pop right off."

Darby was listening, but she snatched a quick look back at Hoku. The filly prowled her fence like an angry cat, glaring after the stallion.

When Jonah turned to see why Darby was so quiet, he must have thought she looked skeptical. He gave a short bark of a laugh.

"You don't believe me? Sometime ask Kimo how many fingers his dad has, that old scoundrel. He's the one tricked me into taking Francie."

They rode a few steps together before Jonah added, "I tell you, that will sure change your vacation in Hawaii, takin' off a thumb."

"Yes," Darby agreed, "I bet it would."

❊ ❊ ❊

By eleven o'clock, Jonah had been teaching Darby to pony for almost an hour.

Sitting on the grass while Kona cropped nearby, Darby decided it was a skill she wasn't likely to master soon. There was so much to keep track of at once.

Two horses, one lead rope, a handful of reins, and her inexperienced riding all had to come together in a kind of synchronized smoothness that made patting your head while rubbing your stomach look easy. And Darby had never been able to do that for more than ten seconds at a time.

Luna had only broken his perfect pace three times—by the candlenut tree, by Hoku's corral, and once in the dip between the hills that Jonah called the fold.

The stallion would probably behave when she took over, Darby thought, if he wasn't provoked.

"Okay, now, before you try it, go up to the house and get yourself some gloves," Jonah told Darby. "They're hanging on a rack in the laundry room."

Darby didn't bother arguing. She started walking, thinking she'd grab a protein bar or something while she was in the house.

"Hey," Jonah asked, "why walk when you can take a horse?"

This time when Darby approached, Kona's gray ears waggled in welcome. Darby still hadn't taken up the stirrups, so she didn't need the sidehill to remount. She smiled when Kona let her settle into the saddle as if they were old friends.

"We'll get you some gloves of your own later," Jonah said, watching her. "Boots, too."

"That's okay," Darby said, gathering her reins.

"What do you mean, 'that's okay'?" Jonah asked.

"I mean, you don't have to do that. Aren't they expensive?"

"Do you want to do this right?" Jonah gestured at the ranch around them.

"Yes, but—"

"And is it possible I know how to outfit you, so that you can grip your reins and ropes and keep your feet from slipping through the stirrups so you won't get dragged to death?"

"I just don't want to cost you a bunch of money." She squeezed her legs against Kona and aimed him toward Sun House.

The gray moved into a long walk, just as she'd hoped, but Darby was still close enough to hear Jonah grumble, "Save me money somewhere else— like on doctor bills."

Chapter 11

"Nobody's eating my pineapple-orange muffins," Auntie Cathy complained as Darby came through the front door of Sun House.

"I am," Darby said, snagging one. As she headed for the laundry room to look for gloves, Darby peeled off the crunchy muffin-top—her favorite part—and munched.

Warmth flooded from the laundry room and Darby heard the *ker-thump*ing of a loaded dryer. She eased inside and closed the door behind her.

It was hot in here, but she set her muffin aside and grabbed the chance to push up her shirtsleeves and fan the hem of her T-shirt.

She should just show everyone the good-luck

charm and dress normally. Or she could take it off. For some reason, she didn't want to do that.

"Some days, I don't even understand myself," Darby muttered.

The muffin's aroma made Darby try to eat it and try on gloves at the same time. It wasn't easy, but she was doing fine until Megan opened the door.

"Hey!" they said simultaneously.

After they'd greeted each other in the same way, at the same moment, Darby and Megan were quiet.

Darby looked down. As usual, Megan's toenails glinted with freshly applied polish, and she wore sandals.

Finally Darby blurted, "Okay, you paid me back by scaring me to death. I thought Francie'd had a heart attack. But I guess I deserved it."

"Yes, you did," Megan said. "But it really *was* an accident."

Megan made a wincing face and said, "That day was just so embarrassing—riding back without you and having to say, 'Oh yeah, Jonah, about your granddaughter? I lost her.' Then I missed my soccer game, and we lost. . . ."

"Thanks for not coming after me," Darby said. She knew Megan was agile enough to have done it. In a scuffle with Megan on a steep, rocky hillside, she would have lost.

"I didn't want to scare Hoku into doing anything crazy," Megan said with a sniff.

"If it hadn't been for her, I would have dragged you back by your ponytail."

They both sighed, and if they'd been friends longer, they might have hugged.

Instead, Megan asked, "Want to go on a ride later?"

"Yeah, can we go back to Crimson Vale?" Darby asked, and when Megan fixed her with a you've-got-to-be-kidding look, Darby added, "I'll be good. I'll do anything you say. I just want to see if we can find that black horse and figure out why he's coming back up here before he causes trouble for Luna." She took a deep breath. "Or Hoku."

"Not you, too," Megan said. "See, this is why I dropped out of the equestrian bit. No one around here just rides. They obsess about horses."

"What do you mean?" Darby asked.

"Jonah. Do you know he spent all night outside with a rifle, so he could—"

"Shoot the Shining Stallion?" Darby finished for her.

"No."

"No?" Darby hadn't asked him directly, but last night he had told her the story of the horse with the marked hoof.

"Well, I'm not positive, but I think he had this weird feeling that Manny might show up and try to take Cade back," Megan said, but then her tone softened. "Manny's a bad guy. I wouldn't wish him on anyone, not even Cade."

Darby wiped sweat from her brow. It was really hot and muggy in here, and what Megan had just said would take some getting used to. Darby wasn't sure she should believe Jonah had been out there with a rifle, waiting for a *man*.

"What made Jonah think he was coming here?"

"I guess about five years ago, before Jonah adopted Cade, Cade's stepdad was doing something illegal in Crimson Vale."

"Jonah said he shot at some horses, but—he still lives in Crimson Vale? Up at the top where Kimo lives, or—"

"Do you think I go visit him?" Megan was exasperated. She twisted her hair up off her neck with one hand and fanned herself with the other. "All I know is a lot of people think he's not really growing taro for a living. No one will say exactly what he does. Or *did*. But whatever it was had the wild horses stirred up.

"My dad said the stallion was out looking for a place to move his herd and that's how he got into a battle with Old Luna."

"And killed him."

"Yeah," Megan said. She wore the cloudy look that came over her when she thought of her father. "My dad and Kimo tried to get Old Luna and the wild horse apart with pitchforks, before Jonah got there."

"So, you really think that last night, Jonah was

out there waiting for Cade's father?" Darby didn't think she could have gotten it right.

"Stepfather," Megan corrected her, "and he's an evil little guy."

"Little?" Darby asked.

"Short," Megan amended. "I only saw him once, the time he came and tried to take Cade back. I was twelve. Jonah made me and Cade hide in his library and lock the door, but before he did, I saw Manny out the window."

Megan wrapped her arms around herself as if, even in the steamy laundry room, the memory chilled her. "Yeah, he's short, but kind of built, you know. Too muscular, like if you only lift weights but don't do anything else?

"Kimo said he was built like a pit bull, but I—" Megan swallowed hard, then gave Darby a self-conscious glance before she went on. "I remember thinking he looked like a fist." Megan gave a shrug. "And his head was like a coconut, all dark and stringy."

Both girls jumped when Auntie Cathy rapped on the laundry-room door.

"Hello? Are you taking a sauna?" Auntie Cathy called. "If you two have a masseuse in there, can I come in?"

Megan opened the door, but turned to Darby and asked, "Have you noticed how weird my mom is?"

Darby put her hands up. She didn't want to get into that discussion.

* * *

Darby worked with Luna until Jonah told her to tie him up at the hitching rack.

"I don't mind leading him back down to his pasture," Darby offered.

She and Luna were building a friendship of sorts. He regarded her with grave acceptance and, probably because she smelled of Hoku, he liked having her near.

"It's good for him to be in the middle of things," Jonah said. "Can't have him turning into a hermit."

He put a neck rope on the stallion and tied him in the center of all the ranch activity.

As Darby and her grandfather walked back to Sun House for lunch, Jonah gave his permission for her to go riding with Megan.

"I wish you'd sit down at the table to eat," Auntie Cathy said, fussing as Jonah and Darby munched peanut-butter sandwiches at the kitchen counter.

"It's a wild-goose chase, you know, looking for that horse," Jonah told Darby. Although she hadn't even mentioned looking for the notched-hoof stallion, he obviously knew she'd be hoping to find him.

"Are you sure it's safe?" Auntie Cathy asked.

"If they don't bring a stud with them, sure," Jonah said.

He ignored Auntie Cathy's you-*know*-that's-not-what-I'm-talking-about stare.

"The three of you must stay together," Auntie

Cathy said. "No excuses."

"Three?" Darby asked.

"And be back by dark," Auntie Cathy insisted, then she looked up at the ceiling as if she could see through to her apartment. "I'll go hurry Meg along."

She left without answering Darby's question, so Darby looked at Jonah.

"Megan and me," Darby counted on her fingers meaningfully.

"Cade goes with you," Jonah said.

"Does he have to?" She lowered her voice and said, "Megan doesn't like Cade. I don't know why, do you?"

"Ask her," Jonah said.

"I did, but she doesn't make sense."

Jonah's only answer was to drink a glass of milk.

"Can't Megan and I just go alone?"

Jonah didn't bring up the last time the two of them had gone into Crimson Vale alone, like Darby expected he would. He just said, "Cade knows Crimson Vale. He grew up there."

Would Cade want to go home while they were there? It didn't seem likely. Still, all the bad stuff she'd heard had been about his stepfather, Manny.

"What about Cade's mother?" Darby asked. "Was it okay with her that you took him in?"

"Dee is a weak woman." Jonah almost spat the words. "She let Manny beat Cade. Think of that," Jonah said in disgust. "She wouldn't stand up to him to protect her own son!"

Darby did think of it. She'd pity the man who hit her when her mother got hold of him. Or her dad. They might not be perfect parents, but they'd defend her with their lives.

"Poor Cade," Darby said.

"You should have seen that boy the day I picked him up." Jonah shook his head at the memory. "Ten years old and he was running away from home, for real. Jaw swollen up like a grapefruit, leading his colt with a belt around its neck. . . . Your *tutu* took care of him, you know." Darby felt a surge of eagerness to meet her great-grandmother, but it was cut off when Jonah added, "While I worked things out with Manny and Dee."

The sly sparkle in Jonah's eye mirrored the expression Cade had used when he'd told her Jonah had had a "talk" with Manny.

Physically, Jonah wasn't a massive man, but he was a leader, Darby thought, and with justice on his side, she'd bet he could be dangerous.

Before they walked back outside, Darby ran to her room, changed into a tank top, and threw a long-sleeved white shirt on over it. She didn't button it, and she was still toying with the idea of pushing her sleeve up and asking Megan where she thought the good-luck charm had come from, once they were riding.

Jonah had waited for her. As they walked, Darby

considered her grandfather and her thoughts veered back to Cade's adoption.

Of course, violence didn't solve anything, but she couldn't help liking the idea that Jonah had shown Cade's stepfather how it felt to be bullied.

Darby glanced back over her shoulder at the sound of Megan's boots tapping downstairs.

"Hey," Darby called as Megan crossed toward her.

"You two be good," Jonah said, veering away from them. He smiled and shook his finger at Megan.

If the older girl rolled her eyes, Darby couldn't tell. Megan wore a baseball cap pulled low enough to touch the top of her sunglasses.

Darby also couldn't read Megan's expression as Cade jogged toward them on Joker. He looked like someone who could hold his own against his mean stepfather.

Cade's luahala hat hid his tight blond braid. His paniolo shirt and a saddle she'd just realized as different from all the others on 'Iolani Ranch made him look older than fifteen.

In minutes, the three of them started on the trail that ran through a ravine that was inaccessible to cars. No one said anything, and Darby thought Cade's manner was steady and resolute. She flashed back on his reaction yesterday, when he'd thought Kimo was questioning his horse sense.

I can tell if a horse is itchin' for a fight, he'd snapped.

But he wouldn't put her and Megan at risk, even if he wanted a face-off with Manny, the stepfather who'd broken his jaw. At least, she was pretty sure he wouldn't.

Chapter 12

I guess I'm the only one who thought this ride would be fun, Darby decided as they headed into the vee-shaped ravine leading to Crimson Vale.

With Cade more serious than usual and Megan looking like she wished she'd never agreed to come along, they affected even the horses' moods. Navigator stayed two strides ahead of Joker and Conch, the grulla Megan rode, but he just plodded along, stirring up the red dust that smelled like cinnamon, without showing off in his leader's position.

"Why's everyone so gloomy?" Darby asked.

"I'm not," Cade and Megan answered in unison.

Darby leaned sideways in her saddle, studying the ground. If they were going to be that way, she'd make her own fun. Still, she wished she'd asked Jonah if it was okay for her to tell Cade and Megan about the mark on the stallion's hoof. But she hadn't, so she wouldn't.

"Which one of you is best at tracking?" Darby asked, to explain her fascination with the dirt.

As if Darby had broken his concentration, Cade's hand jerked on his reins. Joker's hooves scuffed as he scanned the ravine walls and listened with pricked ears.

"Are we tracking something?" Cade asked.

"Of course," Darby said. Despite his protest about not getting involved in "girly gossip," he'd stood right there and talked about this mystery horse.

Sensing Darby's surprise, Cade shrugged. "Jonah just said to keep you two outta trouble."

"Cade," Megan said with false patience, "we're looking for the blue-eyed stallion Darby saw in Crimson Vale. He might be the same horse that was under the candlenut tree, and she thinks if we find out what's got him all stirred up, he'll stay away from the ranch and Hoku won't elope with him."

"I didn't say that!" Darby squeaked, but Megan was almost right. Darby couldn't wait to see a stallion so splendid he'd stirred up a legend. But he'd better stay away from Hoku.

Darby nodded to herself. When she glanced over to see if anyone had noticed, she caught Cade's faint smile.

Now, what was that about? Darby wondered. It was almost as if Cade had teased Megan into talking to him.

Turning her eyes on Megan, Darby saw the other girl's cheeks were flushed. She seemed revitalized by treating Cade like he was simpleminded.

Megan met Darby's gaze, tucked her cherry Coke–colored hair under her baseball cap, and began talking like a tour guide.

"If you ever get stranded out here again," she told Darby, "there's a way to kind of get your bearings. There are lots of ridges, outcroppings, and gullies, but it sort of has three floors.

"The top level's by the highway. There's a turnout where cars can park and a few people walk to the pali overlook. Then there's the middle one. Remember where we were before?" Megan asked. "We had a good view of the whole valley, and we sat in that little cave? And the bottom level is the beach, which you're totally familiar with because that's how you made your getaway."

When Megan stuck her tongue out at her, Darby laughed, then asked, "What about waterfalls?"

"They're all over the place." Megan gestured widely. "When the sun's right, the valley's full of rainbows kind of refracting in halos around them."

Darby was shivering with delight when Cade warned, "I've only seen wild horses at Shining Stallion Falls a couple of times, and there are millions of places for them to hide when they hear us coming."

"*Ker-blam, pitter-patter,*" Darby said, then covered her traitorous mouth before Megan and Cade stared at her.

"What was that?" Megan asked.

The heat of a thousand suns was no hotter than the blush covering her face, Darby thought miserably.

She struggled to explain, "When, uh, somebody was 'raining on our parade,' my friend Heather and I used to, um, say that."

Megan laughed, tilted her head toward Cade, and said, "Yeah, don't rain on Darby's parade."

Darby couldn't remember a time she'd been so humiliated.

Luckily, Megan put an end to the worst of Darby's embarrassment by blurting, "There!"

For an instant, Darby thought Megan had spotted a wild horse, but the other girl was holding her reins in one hand and leaning back in her saddle as she pointed at the ground. Megan pulled Conch to a stop. When the grulla humped up his back and flattened his ears Megan told him, "Don't you even think about it."

Hoofprints marked with glittering mica showed in the red dirt.

Cade reined Joker over close enough to see.

"One horse traveling alone," he said, glancing at Megan.

"I guess," she said.

"If it *is* a stallion, where are his mares?" Darby wondered aloud, but her heart was pounding hard, as she moved Navigator closer, for a better look.

"I don't think we can tell if it's a stallion from his prints," Megan joked.

I can, Darby thought. And then she saw the wavy edge of the hoofprint. The trespassing stallion had passed this way.

"Can you tell how old the print is?" Darby asked.

"I bet Kit could," Cade said. "Tracking is sort of his family hobby."

Darby already knew that, and so did Jonah, so why had he kicked dust over the tracks so Kit couldn't read them? And why had he told Darby to keep the hoofprint a secret?

Could Jonah feel sheepish about sparing the stallion's life? Maybe he didn't want the cowboys to know.

Darby gave up guessing. She had too little experience with guys to know if she struck on the right answer.

The three riders passed a small cave and black rocks Darby recognized. Then they started up a steep trail choked with greenery. And soon Darby heard rushing water.

"We'll let the horses drink at the foot of the falls," Cade shouted as the rushing turned to a roar.

"When we were here before, I didn't hear a waterfall," Darby yelled. She was talking to Megan, but Joker fell in step beside Navigator.

"This one's weird. When we get up there, you'll see the greenery pretty much disappears. When I was a kid, I'd watch storms try to get over that"—Cade pointed at a soaring peak—"highest point on the pali, and it popped them like water balloons. They dropped most of their rain on the ocean side, and only enough for this one waterfall on this side."

Darby thought that sounded interesting, so she urged Navigator forward, trying to ride next to Cade so she could ask questions, but Joker vaulted over six feet of trail and opened his lead over Navigator, so conversation was impossible. Darby looked after them.

Cade had made the Appaloosa surge ahead on purpose, but she couldn't guess why.

They'd all dismounted, loosened their cinches, and let their horses crowd around the foamy pool at the base of the waterfall when, without thinking, Darby took off her white shirt and tied it around her waist.

Megan had just used her hands to scoop water to her mouth and Darby was reaching past her to do the same when Megan uttered a gasp that sounded like something ripping.

"What?" Cade asked, but then he stared at Darby's wrist, too.

"Megan?" Darby asked as the older girl backed away.

"Take it off!" Megan ordered. "Now! Darby, I'm not joking."

"This?" Darby asked, touching the braids tied around her wrist.

That was all it took for Megan to slide-tackle Darby off her feet and jerk the bracelet free.

It didn't fly very far.

Panting in amazement, Darby stared at the trinket. It had fallen on a rock at the edge of the pool. It sat there, totally harmless.

"What did you th-think it was?" Darby tried to control her shaky voice.

"I know what it is," Cade said.

"So do I," Megan said. "Sorry."

As Megan rolled away from Darby and regained her footing, she still sounded troubled.

"Well, *I* don't know what it is!" Darby said. "I mean, beyond horsehair and—"

"Not horsehair," Megan corrected her.

Darby felt a chill from the way she said it.

"It's a *lei niho palaoa*, or part of one," Cade said. "Those braids are made of human hair."

"So?" Darby said. She tried to sound casual, but now she was in no hurry to pick it up.

"We saw one at the Bishop Museum in Honolulu," Megan said. "The braids of human hair are tied with coconut fiber and the one we saw had a shell hook in the middle."

"I think it used to have one," Darby said faintly.

"Did you break it?" Cade accused, as if she'd splashed red paint on the *Mona Lisa*.

"Where did you get it?" Megan asked at the same time.

With a sigh, Darby explained what she thought had happened.

She told them how she'd climbed down the rocks to Hoku and the necklace had looped over her instep and tripped her.

Frowning, Megan met Cade's eyes, then said, "Go on."

"I fell, but I guess while I was swimming the shell hook snagged on my jeans and then they were so wrecked when I got back to Sun House, I just kicked them off, and finally, when I was going to wash them . . ." Darby shrugged. "There it was. I thought it looked like a cool old thing, so I kept it."

"It's old, all right," Cade said. "If you'd worn it into town, you could've been accused of trafficking in antiquities."

Both girls stared at Cade, surprised at his authoritative voice.

"It's sacred," Cade said, "to the *ali'i*—a member of royalty," he explained to Darby, "for whom it was made." The *ali'i* had them made out of their own hair and it was a sign of rank and protection."

"I thought it was hair from the *mother* of the *ali'i*," Megan said.

"But the point is, it's a good-luck charm, right?"

Darby asked. "That's all I was doing with it, though it sure hasn't worked for me."

Darby gave a short laugh, but Cade and Megan didn't join in. They stared at her as if they were recalling the fainting goat, Luna's thirst, and the possible return of a killer stallion.

"It's *kapu*, you know—*forbidden*—for anyone to touch it except the person it was made for, so if I was superstitious, I'd say it was working just like it's supposed to." Megan kept her voice steady, but after she'd finished, she held the fingers of one hand over her mouth.

"Do you guys *believe* in this?" Darby demanded. "That it's cursed?"

She looked down at the little black and brown amulet.

"No," Cade and Megan said together, and relief rushed over Darby.

"But she could probably get arrested, don't you think?" Megan asked Cade.

"Arrested!" Darby squeaked.

"For grave robbing," Cade said.

"Oh, no. No way," Darby said, flashing her hands in front of her as if she could erase everything. "I didn't even pick it up. *It* glommed onto *me*. And I haven't been near any graves."

A bird's raucous call came loud enough to be heard over the falls, before Megan said, "Well, actually, you have."

Darby followed Megan's glance toward the pali, then stared as if she could see through to the other side where the mouths of caves faced the sea.

Kimo—and Megan, too—had told her that dead *ali'i* were hidden there. "Volunteers" had been lowered on ropes from the top, cradling remains in royal wrappings, treasured possessions, and food for the journey to the afterlife. They arranged everything in reverent rituals, then sacrificed themselves to keep the burial caves secret.

"Grave robbing is a big deal," Megan said. "It's in the news whenever it happens because some people think the bones and artifacts should be left right where they are, so that—uh—the spirits are undisturbed, or whatever. And some think the stuff should be in museums, where they can be studied and appreciated, instead of chancing our ancestors' bones to grave robbers who'll sell them on eBay."

Cade looked nervous as he said, "They go to black-market collectors."

"How do you know so much about this?" Megan demanded.

"I pay attention," Cade snapped, but he took his hat off and held it in both hands, staring at the intricate meshing of brown and beige, not looking at the girls.

"We'd better get out of here," Megan said, rubbing her arms.

"I don't think Manny's involved in any of that

stuff." Cade's head was still bent over the hat in his hands. The center part in his blond hair was ruler-straight. "Not anymore."

Darby grew very still, but her mind went whirling. Could Cade's stepfather's illegal business be grave robbing? What if he traded in ancient treasures and it was the criminal buyers coming and going from the caves that had stirred up the wild horses?

That was possible, wasn't it? She couldn't get up the courage to ask, but she let the possibility take shape in her mind while the waterfall rushed, and then Megan's eyes caught hers.

Is that what Megan had meant when she'd said, *You don't know what he's capable of,* about Cade? Had he helped his stepfather *traffic in antiquities*? But Cade had come to live with Jonah when he was just ten.

Oh boy, Darby thought, releasing a breath she didn't know she'd been holding. *This is not good.*

"He *was,* and he had me guard a cave one night. I had a flashlight, but—" Cade turned his hat by its brim. When he spoke next, he sounded ashamed. "No one ever explained to me about shark's teeth decorations, or dogs' teeth embedded in clubs, and how they used to cremate the bodies and just wrap the bones—"

Darby had managed to convince herself that Cade, as a little kid, had imagined those things, until Megan held up a hand to silence Cade. Then she gave him a stern look.

"Cade, my dad used to tell me stories to try to help me understand my roots, my heritage, you know? I kind of understand the old way. In fact, I think that stuff is cool, but you still wouldn't get me—even now—to stay in any cave all alone at night, let alone one with the bones of the ancestors."

Darby felt a warmth for Megan she hadn't before. Even though Megan didn't like Cade for some reason, it was clear she sympathized.

"Anyway," Cade said, "I got scared and sneaked out of the cave before whoever was coming for things got there, and that's when Manny beat me up pretty good."

"Pretty bad," Darby corrected, without meaning to.

Cade gave a *whatever* shrug, but Darby sat close enough to see the bulge in his cheek as his tongue probed the spot that had been broken and swollen.

"But then Jonah had a talk with Manny." Cade sounded proud that his adopted father had defended him.

"So, if Manny's out of the business now," Darby said briskly, "that necklace probably fell there a long time ago. Maybe because it was broken, they left it behind?"

"It would still be worth plenty," Cade said. "But I guess it could have happened that way, or maybe a bird got into a cave and pecked at the shiny shell, then flew away with it and let it fall to see if there was food inside."

All at once the mourning voices from Darby's dream came back to her. She thought of the sad women sitting in a cave, holding their hands out to her.

They'd been reaching for the necklace.

Darby bolted to her feet.

Of course she wanted to see the wild stallion, but he was obviously hiding. Since he was, she wanted to get away from that necklace. Far, far away, as fast as she could.

"Let's get out of here," Darby said.

"We will," Cade said resolutely. "Just as soon as we put that necklace back where it came from."

Chapter 13

"*What* are you talking about?" Darby asked in bewilderment, but Cade spoke right over her.

"Some people feel awfully strongly about this," he said to Megan. "I say we put it back until it can be blessed by the proper religious leader, and then it can be moved to a museum."

"That's an okay plan. All except that last part," Megan said. "Once it's blessed and returned to the *ali'i*, the cave should be sealed."

"So someone can just come *un*seal it all over again?" Cade demanded.

"Stop! Couldn't it be like a replica or something?" Darby turned toward Megan. "You said yourself tourists and hikers come into Crimson Vale. Besides,

I don't want to keep it. Let's turn it in to the police or something!"

Megan's head tilted to one side as if she was considering the idea.

"You girls ride back to the ranch," Cade said. "I'll take care of it."

"Oh, yeah. Right." Megan stood with her hands on her hips and feet wide apart. To Darby, she looked like an Amazon warrior. "Should we put on white gloves and have a little tea party, too?"

Cade burst into laughter that seemed, to Darby, totally inappropriate for the mess they were in.

But Cade kept laughing until finally he cleared his throat to say, "You are such a jock. I suppose *you* want to put it back."

"No, I don't. The idea scares the heck out of me — not the climbing, but the cave. And I'm not too crazy about carrying that thing, either." Megan flashed a doubtful look at the necklace. "But it's the right thing to do, so I'll help."

"What about me?" Darby asked. Megan and Cade stared at her with such astonishment, she had to explain. "I'm the one who got us into this in the first place, and I've already climbed down there before."

"Yeah, I know," Megan said, pointing to Darby's bruised cheek.

"One slip. Except for that I did fine," Darby insisted.

Cade stood with both hands on his saddle, muttering about his rope.

He must have forgotten it, Darby thought. Maybe he'd give up on this foolhardy plan.

"Too bad you don't have it," Darby said.

"Have—my rope? I've got my riata," he said, lifting a braided leather coil. "I don't go anywhere without it, but I don't think we'll need it from here."

Cade and Megan decided they were going down a path he remembered, leaving Darby at the base of the waterfall with the horses.

"Why don't I get any say in this?" Darby tried not to sound like what she was, the youngest of the group.

Megan gave Darby's shoulder a gentle punch.

"We know the territory better. That's all," Megan said.

"*I* know the territory," Cade contradicted her. "But I've seen Mekana go like a gecko up the side of a waterfall."

Divided over whether she should yell at Cade for using her dad's name for her, or acknowledge his compliment about her climbing, Megan hesitated, which gave Darby an opening to distract them.

"You two are stronger and in better shape than I am," Darby conceded, "but if you get in trouble, I'm smart enough to get you out of it."

"Of course, there's that, too," Megan said, smiling.

And so they left her, bickering as they followed a

maze of thread-wide trails and tiny handholds that Cade remembered from his childhood.

At first Darby watched over the edge, but it didn't take long before they vanished from sight. Listening to the crunch of their boots on the rocks and watching the cascades of sand plummet hundreds of feet to the beach below just made her nervous, anyway.

After she had walked from horse to horse, loosening Joker's breast collar, rubbing under Conch's headstall until he groaned with pleasure, then working her hand between Navigator's saddle pad and his withers to knead his muscles, Darby decided to take her boots off and dangle her feet in the waterfall pool.

Darby caught her breath. Surprised, she yanked her feet out of the pool, which was definitely the coldest substance she'd felt in Hawaii. Gradually, though, she rolled her jeans up to her knees and soaked her feet some more.

She gazed into the silver curtain of water, noticing white streaks where it touched the rocks behind it, black streaks where it appeared to plummet past darkness. Could there be a cave behind the waterfall? She tried to picture such a thing and decided she must have seen it in a movie.

She'd been sitting poolside, trying to decide if the waterfall had been in *Peter Pan* or *The Little Mermaid*, when she heard a rustling noise.

Darby thought of the black boar Megan had seen when they'd ridden up here before, but it was probably just a breeze in the flapping ti leaves. Auntie Cathy had told her they were sometimes used to make hula skirts and they were pretty easy to recognize.

But would that sound make all three geldings break off their doze to stare across the valley and up to a ridge?

Good, Darby thought. *Whatever was moving was far away.*

Without Megan and Cade, she didn't feel so brave.

Navigator uttered a shivery nicker that carried across the clearing and out over the valley to the far ridge. Something had been moving, but now it stopped to listen.

It was then that Darby spotted the wild stallion.

He was so far away, her hand could have blocked him from view. But she wouldn't have done such a thing. The black horse was amazing.

From here, Darby couldn't see his blue eye, but his sleek coat and sturdy conformation gave him away. He moved with a stallion's bravado, and though he'd been still when she'd spotted his face among the ferns on her first day on Wild Horse Island, she recognized him. And she'd bet he was the same horse that had stood in the shadows of the candlenut tree, the same stallion who'd killed Old Luna and survived to run free.

He was running now, and though Darby knew

that horses sometimes galloped for the sheer joy of it, she didn't get that feeling. Desperation charged each of his strides.

Conch pulled back against his tether. Megan had tied the grulla up short, because he was young and reacted to everything, but now he'd turned his attention to a figure behind the wild horse.

Darby wished she had binoculars. She tried to puzzle out what was behind the black horse, but only one guess made sense: a man.

Darby couldn't have said why she was so certain it was Manny, but something—location, of course, and all the talk about Manny and wild horses—told Darby it was him.

A small avalanche slid and tumbled nearby.

Darby had always thought "I nearly jumped out of my skin" was a silly, exaggerated expression. Until now.

Megan's voice soared up from the face of the pali, shouting "We're fine!" and knocking Darby breathless.

Darby dropped to her knees and scuttled over to the edge. She didn't want Megan attracting Manny's attention.

"Shh," Darby hissed, over the edge.

Waves broke on the beach below, and if they covered her voice, Darby thought, they'd definitely hide Megan's. And though Manny couldn't possibly hear from where he was, unless he had radar like a bat,

Darby didn't want to take a chance.

"I said, don't worry your pretty little head, because we're safe," Megan yelled even louder.

Megan was in great spirits, Darby thought.

"Okay," Darby whispered back.

"Guess she can't hear me," Megan called to Cade.

Darby heard Cade mumble something in response and she crossed her fingers that Megan wouldn't use her soccer-field shout to announce her whereabouts to Darby again.

If she did, Darby didn't hear her. Gradually the tension drained out of Darby's muscles.

By the time she edged back to the pool, the geldings had lost interest in the ridgeline. It was empty of horse and man, and so were the rows of taro planted between channels of blue water. Darby hoped it would stay that way.

Then she heard something nearby that didn't sound like Megan or Cade. It was moving this way too fast to be them.

Darby closed her eyes to concentrate on what sounded like high heels going up a parking garage stairwell. Since that was ridiculous, she stood up and walked around barefoot, tilting her head from side to side, using her eyes as well as her ears as she tried to locate the source of the sound.

No bushes were waving from an animal's passage. No branches bounced under the weight of a bird. And the wind was taking a break.

The tapping sound stopped, but Darby felt the tension of something focused on her awareness. Whatever it was hadn't gone away. It was waiting for her to move.

Darby shivered, wishing she had a less vivid imagination.

I won't think about that, she told herself. Don't remember that some civilizations sacrificed beloved horses to go along with their masters into the netherworld.

Could the Shining Stallion story have grown out of such a tradition? Could one of the stallions that had been sacrificed, have refused to go easily into the darkness? And what if he lingered here, making spooky stallion sounds inside the soaring cliffs?

Get real, Darby scolded herself.

Nothing like that was possible, of course, but Darby decided she'd feel more comfortable alongside the horses. Three tons of living horseflesh should be able to protect her from a ghost.

Darby didn't stop to pull on her boots. Barefooted, she picked her way across the red dirt. She'd only taken a few steps, but if she'd stayed where she'd been standing, the blue-eyed stallion might have crushed her.

A haunted scream burst from the stallion's mouth as he plunged through the waterfall, surrounded by a ring of rainbows and crystal spray.

As a group, the geldings shifted away from him,

slamming shoulders and stirrups against one another, leaving Darby exposed to the stallion's fury.

"I'm not the one," she told him shakily. "I won't hurt you."

Vibrating with fury, the black horse bared his teeth and rose in a half rear. As he came down, just feet from Darby, dripping feathers showed on his trim legs and the ground quaked under hooves that left wet prints like blood in the red dirt. Knots and tangles studded his mane. Thorns and a twig of green berries hung snarled in his wet tail.

He was a wild beast, Darby thought, glittering with water from the fall named for him, but she tried to encompass him with all her horse charmer's instincts.

He was magnificent, screaming his outrage that she'd followed him here. This place of wild beauty belonged to those with wings or tails. Not to her.

Navigator whinnied, and he couldn't have told Darby to flee more clearly than if he'd shouted "Run!"

The stallion answered Navigator's defiance with a sound her ears couldn't take in. The neigh's shrill thunder drowned out the rush of the waterfall.

Should she back up, or go forward? Darby didn't know how to obey the stallion. She pictured Hoku, charging the fence with flattened ears when Luna passed by.

But I'm not a horse, Darby thought. *I don't know how*

to deflect a stallion's attack.

The geldings did.

Brown, gray, and bronze heads bowed to the screaming stallion and he went silent. The geldings lowered their muzzles to brush the ground and rolled their eyes, telling the black horse he was the unquestioned ruler of this place.

At last the stallion settled on all four hooves. He snorted as rivulets ran off his onyx shoulders and down his legs, turning the dust into scarlet mud.

With the three geldings' submission assured, the stallion turned back to Darby.

One brown eye and one blue fixed on Darby's. The stallion's stare was hypnotic. If he could read her mind, he'd find only awe.

And confusion.

Should she lower her eyes as the geldings had?

No. Darby jerked her chin up to the height of her neck and strained each vertebra away from the next. Instinct told her not to cower before the mighty horse.

Just then, rocks slid and stones ricocheted off the cliff. Cade and Megan were coming back up.

Before she could shout out to her friends she glimpsed hands, and Cade's face came into view.

As the stallion turned on this new challenge, Darby caught the sapphire flash of his eye. With a seesaw buck and a deadly lashing of his hind hooves, the stallion threatened the intruders and bolted past

Darby and the geldings.

His hard wet hooves clattered, seeking balance on a slick rock shelf, and Darby ran after him, dreading a fall for either of them.

Safe and out of reach of human hands, he galloped with slanting steps down the path and toward the ravine, a shining black mustang in a halo of red dust.

Chapter 14

Darby stumbled back in the direction of the waterfall. She'd never been so eager to put on socks and boots, which just proved the wild stallion must exude some kind of mind control. Otherwise she couldn't have ignored the pain.

Cade rushed to meet Darby, not to sympathize with the way she limped on both feet at the same time, but to marvel over the stallion.

"Manny told me I made him up." Cade's frown was mixed with an expression of wonder. "And then, after I got older, I thought he was dead."

"What do you mean?" Darby asked.

"You know, the stallion that fought Old Luna,"

Cade said. "The one Jonah killed."

If she was going to tell Cade the truth, Darby thought, this was the time to do it. But it was Jonah's secret.

"Isn't he incredible! Where did he come from?" Cade asked. He looked over both shoulders as if the horse had left some sign.

Darby had the weirdest feeling her world had gone as still as a movie freeze-frame. A lot depended on what she said next, and even though the stallion hadn't sworn her to silence, she wasn't about to tell Cade or anyone else about the ringing of hooves on stone, just before the stallion burst through the waterfall.

"Just sort of out of nowhere," Darby said, and that was no lie. "I was over talking to Navigator and when I turned around, the stallion was charging me."

It was no use trying to describe the horse's wild beauty, his halo of rainbow droplets, or the fierceness that left her convinced he was the horse who'd been locked in a bloody battle with Luna's sire. Besides, Cade was as enchanted with the stallion as she was.

"You saw the Shining Stallion without me?" Megan coughed against the powdery earth that coated her face as she pulled herself back up and over the ledge. She didn't say anything about Cade beating her to the top, but she looked at him in surprise.

And though Darby caught Megan's amazed

expression, Cade didn't. He was still staring after the wild horse.

"I used to call him Black Lava," Cade said.

Dark and deadly, burning with power. Darby sighed at the rightness of the name, and as she did, she looked down and saw a distinctive hoofprint in the dirt. Smudged and half-hidden by Cade's boot, it had one wavy edge.

"What are we going to do about—" Megan began, but Cade's voice stopped her.

"I thought he was dead because of the skull," he said.

"What skull?" Darby asked, not sure she really wanted to know.

"Manny found this horse skull washed up in a cove. And about the same time, this wild horse herd I'd been following around the valley"—Cade paused to gesture at the terrain around them—"just dropped out of sight."

Then he tried to erase his wistful tone by changing it to rough sarcasm. "Punctured the bone right between the eye sockets," Cade said, using his index finger to make a drilling motion in the middle of his forehead. He gave an uneasy laugh, too, but anybody could tell he didn't think it was funny.

"The skull couldn't be from the horse Jonah shot," Darby said reasonably, but she was thinking that when Jonah had told her about Manny shooting at horses in his taro patch, she'd thought he'd meant shooting to frighten them off, not kill them.

Without meaning to, she studied the hoofprint Cade was standing on.

Knock it off, she told herself and darted her eyes over to the rainbow, then tilted her head to one side in fake concentration.

"You look just like an owl when you do that," Megan said.

"Do what? Think?" Darby demanded, but then she waved Megan's explanation away and told Cade, "The time's not right. Didn't you come to the ranch pretty soon after the stallions fought?"

"Yeah," Cade said. "What's that got to do with—"

"She has a point." Megan seconded Darby's idea. "The closest cove to 'Iolani is miles away and, not to be gross, a horse's body would still have had plenty of skin and—oh." Megan stopped herself and grimaced. "I suppose something could have been eating it."

"Like what?" Darby asked. "I thought there weren't any big predators on this island."

"Wild dogs?" Megan suggested, but then her tone and expression hardened. "And boars."

"All I know," Cade cut in, "is that the skull is nailed over Manny's door. If you have the bad sense to go over there, you can see it."

"No thanks," Darby said.

It was unlike her to feel so scared. Stories of

menehune and tsunami horses and ghost stallions grazing among graves didn't frighten her, but the man
who'd broken Cade's jaw and surely shot the horse
whose head hung over his doorway was no myth.

She never wanted to meet up with him.

Megan and Cade must have felt much the same
way, because they tightened their horses' gear,
mounted, and rode back the way they'd come without
another word.

They were ten minutes into their ride back to
'Iolani Ranch when Megan asked, "So what shall we
do about the necklace? We didn't really decide."

"You didn't leave it there?" Darby yelped, pulling
Navigator to a stop. "I'm not taking it home with me."

"You don't have to. I've got it," Cade said.

"But why didn't you leave it there?" Darby asked.

"We couldn't," Megan said, giving Cade a glare.

"It's my fault," Cade agreed. "I kind of forgot the
part where the caves are sealed with boulders and I
was ten years old the last time I slipped inside one."

Small enough to ease through a narrow opening
and hand things out, Darby thought. That's why his
stepfather had made a child part of his dirty work. To
anyone who checked, the entrance to the sacred cave
would look undisturbed. Manny wouldn't go to jail
and he clearly didn't care about anyone else, includ-
ing his stepson.

Cade must have known, even as a little kid, that he was doing something wrong, Darby thought, and she'd bet that was why he was so determined to set things right now.

"But you think you found the right cave, after all this time?" Darby asked.

"I think so, but I'd have to go inside to be positive," Cade said.

"I almost squeezed through. . . ."

"Why are you looking at me like that?" Darby asked Megan.

Both Cade and Megan, in fact, considered Darby as if lining her up against a mental tape measure.

"Like what?" Cade said slowly.

"Like you were sizing me up for a ready-made coffin," Darby snapped.

Megan shook her head as if she could dislodge the idea that had shown so clearly in her eyes. "No, we're not going to let you go back down there. The footing's too unstable. And, honestly? Little as you are, I still don't think you're the size of a ten-year-old boy."

"Thanks, I guess," Darby said, but her relief was mixed with uneasiness. "Don't you think we should leave it in the valley? Maybe eventually we should turn it over to a museum like Cade thinks, or put it back in a cave, but one thing I know for sure is that I don't want anyone else, uh, deciding for us."

"Where would you leave it?" Cade asked, looking

back over his shoulder.

"I saw a little hidey-hole," Darby said, but she was thinking that if the stallion hid behind the waterfall, it would have to be a safe place.

"A hidey-hole?" Megan asked skeptically.

Darby nodded. "I'll just ride back and—"

"I don't think so," Megan said, hitting each word with sledgehammer emphasis.

"You can trust me now," Darby promised. "You guys sit right here and count to—"

"No way!" Megan said loudly, and Darby couldn't really blame her.

They rode in silence. Any camaraderie she thought she'd seen between Megan and Cade had evaporated. In fact, they acted colder to each other now than before.

Darby kept looking at shadows around rocks, between trees, trying to memorize her surroundings. Nothing was going to keep her from returning the artifact to Crimson Vale. Even if she stashed it in the wrong cave, it would be safer there than at 'Iolani Ranch.

She should probably tell Jonah about the necklace. Wouldn't the Hawaiian horse charmer know someone qualified to apologize to the ancestors and explain about the necklace?

Every rustle and crack in the vegetation around them made her jump.

"This is what I get for having a good imagination," Darby explained when Megan finally gave her a quizzical look. "I feel like we're being watched."

"It's quiet," Megan said in a creepy voice. "Too quiet."

Darby was laughing when she heard a whine, just like a bullet's ricochet in a cowboy movie, and then she heard galloping hooves.

All three of them looked at each other.

"It's Manny," Cade said calmly.

"If it is—" Megan began.

"It is," Cade repeated.

Was he shooting at wild horses or trying to spook *them* into running? Darby wondered.

"*If* it is," Megan repeated, "just let us do the talking."

Cade didn't bother to answer, but his *yeah, right* expression told Darby that five years hadn't been enough time for Cade to forgive his stepfather.

"He doesn't have any grudges against me or Darby," Megan insisted, but Darby could tell she wasn't getting through to him.

Cade wasn't the child he'd been. Now he was a young man, and he wanted to confront his stepfather.

"Give it to me," Darby said, holding out her hand for the broken necklace.

Cade frowned. Megan sounded bewildered as she asked, "What do you think Manny's going to do,

Darby? Frisk us for something he doesn't even know we have?"

"All I know is if Manny's doing the shooting, he's after Black Lava for some reason. It can't be easy, chasing down a wild horse on foot."

"What makes you think he's on foot? He's as lazy as he is mean," Cade said.

She didn't blurt that she'd seen a man stalking Black Lava on a ridge across from the waterfall, because then she'd have to admit she'd heard the horse behind the waterfall.

"I'd just feel better if it was in *my* pocket," Darby said. She dropped her reins and crossed her arms. If they thought she was being bratty, so what?

Cade and Megan consulted each other silently and finally Megan shrugged.

Cade reached under his saddle's skirt, removed the necklace from a pouch, then reined Joker close to Navigator and handed over the necklace. Darby thought his fingers parted from it with reluctance.

As soon as she took it, the braids curled into her palm like a cat that wanted to be petted.

That's only imagination, Darby thought, but her hand jerked back and she dropped the artifact on the ground between the two horses' hooves.

"Sorry. I'll get it," she said, and before either of the others could dismount, she did.

On the ground, she was more aware of Conch

pawing and Joker's flared nostrils. The Appaloosa tested the air with worried sniffs and Navigator didn't want to approach him.

Did Joker remember the smell of Cade's stepfather? Darby wondered.

"Should we stop or keep riding?" Darby asked.

The phrase *sitting duck* crossed her mind as she pulled gently on her reins, trying to lead Navigator close enough to pick up the necklace.

"I'm not moving until we know what's up," Megan said. "There's high growth on both sides of the trail and the footing's uneven. Whoever's firing that gun might get excited and mistake us for whatever he's shooting at."

Conch lowered his head and pawed more vigorously, anxious to move on, but Megan didn't let him go.

"Do you think Manny's shooting at Black Lava?" Darby asked Cade. She knew it was a mistake as soon as the name cleared her lips. What had made her ask such a thing?

"Don't ask me to think like him," Cade said. "He doesn't do it very often, and when he does, it means trouble. Look, do you want me to get that for you?"

"I'll get it," Darby insisted.

"Get what?"

She didn't know where the voice came from, but a branch broke on the left side of the trail, just ahead.

Cold. Frozen in place, Darby had no words for how scared she was, but she swooped down to grab the necklace and shoved it into her pocket with clumsy fingers as Manny stepped into the path before them.

He was grinning like a hyena, Darby thought.

He wore a faded Hawaiian shirt open over khaki shorts. Heavy boots were laced up his shins. He was not much taller than she was, about five-foot-four inches tall, Darby guessed. And even though Manny was afoot and Cade was mounted, the man seemed bigger when his eyes locked on Cade's.

He was the first Hawaiian Darby had encountered who didn't radiate welcome.

After taking in Cade's ease in his paniolo saddle, Manny said, "You kids see a horse come through here?"

His voice was higher-pitched than Darby had expected.

Even though Megan and Cade were right here, she didn't like being alone on the ground with Manny.

Megan and Cade had both shaken their heads "no" to Manny's question, but Darby backed away from him, leading Navigator to a rock where she could remount.

Go away, Darby thought. If the man had a single

nerve in his body, he must feel their feelings shoving at him.

"How about you?" Manny asked.

"Me?" Darby squeaked. She glanced at Manny and saw his rifle barrel rested on his shoulder as he walked toward her. Was the necklace in her pocket sending out a beacon Manny could follow?

"Nope," Darby managed. She held her reins in her sweating hand, grabbed a piece of Navigator's mane, and put her boot on top of a rock.

She was about to pull herself up into the saddle when Manny said, "I see you don't have no trouble keeping your mouth shut now."

Darby looked in time to see Manny, sluggish as a python, shift his attention to Cade. Darby did the same. With surprise, she saw Cade's eyes looked hazy and disinterested under the brim of his hat.

Darby felt oddly proud of him for keeping calm.

I see you don't have no trouble keeping your mouth shut now. He was actually bragging about breaking a little boy's jaw.

When the meaning of Manny's words hit her, Darby missed her attempt to step into her stirrup and she couldn't help watching as Manny took a strutting step toward Cade's horse and asked, "Don't have no message for your mom?"

There. Cade's eyes showed a spark of hurt, and Manny laughed as if he'd scored a point.

Cade drew a deep breath, and all at once, as creeped-out as she felt, Darby knew that if there was a time to play dumb, this was it.

"Hey, I'm Darby Carter," she drawled, as if she were from South Carolina instead of Southern California.

Despite her revulsion, she led Navigator a few steps closer to Manny and presented her hand for shaking. She really would rather have touched a python, but she couldn't let Cade get pulled into an argument with his stepfather.

Darby doubted it would stop with words, and after that, it wouldn't be a fair fight.

"Jonah is my grandfather!" she announced so loudly, a colorful bird left a treetop. "How are you? I mean, *aloha*! Everyone around here is just so friendly."

From the corner of her eye, Darby caught Megan staring at her in astonishment, but she ignored the older girl. Instead, Darby grinned until the corners of her mouth threatened to split. It took that long for Manny to reach out with a suspicious smile and shake her hand.

For one awful moment, Darby thought he might jerk her closer to him, but she kept a mindless grin on her lips and hoped it was true about angels protecting fools and children.

"Let me give you a leg up," Manny said, nodding at Navigator.

"Huh?" Darby asked.

Manny stood with his shoulder next to Navigator's, facing the gelding's swishing tail.

"Put your boot here," Manny said, making a cradle of his hands. "Just step there and throw your leg over the saddle."

Darby had hated touching Manny's hand, and giving him control of her foot seemed even worse, but she saw Megan make a tiny nod, as if it was okay.

"Thanks," Darby said, but what if he unlaced his fingers and dropped her? She couldn't help testing his hands before she vaulted up.

Even though Manny stood there, hands on hips, staring up at her as she organized her reins, Darby could still feel the grip of his hands around her boot.

"I didn't know Jonah had a granddaughter," Manny said, then gritted his teeth.

After a full minute, Megan said, "We'd better be—"

But Manny had turned on Cade to say, "Guess the joke's on you, huh, cakey?"

At least that's what it sounded like to Darby, until she remembered Megan had told her that *keiki* meant "child."

"Yeah, *hanai* or not, you won't be inheriting that ranch," Manny said to Cade.

Cade shrugged, but Darby got the feeling Manny had lit the fuse to Cade's anger and it wouldn't be long before he exploded if one of them didn't do something quick.

"Hey! You weren't shooting at that horse you're looking for, were you?" Darby asked.

"Trying to keep 'im out of my taro fields," Manny said. "They eat everything in sight."

"Don't they belong to someone?" Darby asked, trying to sound simpleminded. "Doesn't anybody care about them?"

"Out here, away from the tourists," he said with a sly smile, "it's pretty much every man for himself. And every horse," he said, chuckling. "In fact, it's not exactly safe for you kids. Someone looking through the trees might mistake your horses for wild ones and pop 'em right between the eyes."

Thinking of the skull Cade had described, Darby felt sick.

"That would mean *someone* wasn't very careful," Megan said, and Darby couldn't believe Megan was baiting him into a fight.

"It would," Manny admitted. He pretended to look sad. "And what a shame if your family had another tragedy." He flashed a gloating look at Cade. "Me and Dee, yeah, we felt so bad about Ben's death."

Why, if he was talking about Megan's father, didn't he look at her? And if Manny was really expressing his condolences, why did he sound more like he was making a threat?

Darby felt sweaty and unsteady. The necklace seemed to be trying to make its presence known. It pounded like a pulse in her pocket, and then like a drumbeat. It was a miracle that Manny wasn't staring at her, demanding she turn the artifact over to him.

"My grandfather will be looking for me," Darby said, nudging Navigator with her heels. "So I'd better get home."

Once she had ridden past Manny, she turned and flapped a hand in good-bye. "Aloha!" she shouted again.

Darby tried to sit loosely in the saddle. After all, Manny wasn't about to shoot them in the back. That kind of thing might happen in movies, but not in real life.

The three of them rode on and Darby felt as if a laser beam was aimed between her shoulder blades. Manny was looking after them, for sure. And something told her they shouldn't be riding three abreast.

She drew rein and fell in behind Cade. If any of them were in danger, it would be him. She hadn't looked at Manny's gun. Did it have some kind of superscope projecting a target on her back?

All at once, as if her morbid fantasy had come true, Darby heard a gunshot.

"Sorry," Manny shouted as all three of them twisted in their saddles to look back at him pointing his rifle skyward. "Just saw a little something I wanted to take home for dinner."

She didn't see anything fall from the sky, but all the way home, Darby imagined the dying flutter of feathers.

Chapter 15

"Manny said there was no law to make him stop shooting the wild horses," Darby told Jonah when she found him inspecting Luna's corral.

"You've done a good job here," her grandfather said.

Looking for horse manure wasn't what she'd had in mind when Jonah told her he'd talk with her about the encounter with Manny.

"Thank you," Darby said. "He told me it was every man—and horse—for himself."

"He's right," Jonah said. "Even though the wild horses are part of the old Hawaii—a story you should get your *tutu*, not me, to tell you—they've been getting into homesteads and causing problems the last twenty years or so. Too many people."

"That's not the horses' fault," Darby said.

"He didn't bother you kids?" Jonah asked, his brown eyes narrowing as his voice got quiet. "Threaten you in any way?"

Other than taunting Cade, what had he done? Cold menace had flowed from him, and Darby wanted to make sure the necklace didn't fall into his hands, but she'd be lying if she said he'd done anything threatening.

"He didn't do anything to us," Darby admitted, "but how can we stop him—"

"If he comes on our place, we'll stop him," Jonah said adamantly.

"But the black horse, the one that might be the Shining Stallion—"

"That black horse has had his second chance," Jonah said. "He's on strike three."

Darby knew what he meant. As a sire, Luna was more important than all the other horses of the ranch put together.

"We're one of the few working ranches in the islands these days," Jonah said. "I could sell these two thousand acres for a million dollars each to build houses on, and that's a lot of money."

"It is," Darby agreed, but her eyes skimmed the green velvet of the hills, thinking it would be sacrilege to cover them with houses.

"But I can't put a price tag on heritage that goes

back a thousand years," Jonah said with a shrug. "What number should I write? How many zeroes would I add to make up for selling soil powdered with my ancestors' bones? *Our* ancestors," he corrected himself. "And all our *mana*—our spirit and good fortune—comes from our ancestors. I'll tell you what, I'll grab the bulldozers' blades with my bare hands before I let anyone turn this ranch into a mall and parking lot. I'll come back to haunt any of my heirs that do the same, too. I'm not pranking you, Granddaughter."

"I'd never give up 'Iolani Ranch for houses," Darby said, insulted.

"And you understand that Luna is the cornerstone of our Quarter Horse breeding program, so I can't let that blue-eyed black have a chance at him," Jonah said, circling back to his point.

"I understand," Darby said.

"Humph," Jonah said. "We'll see."

Darby hid the ancient necklace inside her dictionary-diary. Every time she thought of it, she sucked her stomach in so hard, it hurt. She woke each morning for a week, from dreams of dark, echoing caves, and she thought she must be grinding her teeth in her sleep, because her jaw ached.

All week, she watched for the black horse—on ridgelines, in folds between the hills, out at the border of Pearl Pasture. If she glimpsed him first, she'd scare him away before Jonah or Luna spotted him.

But the wild stallion didn't appear under the candlenut tree at night, or come to the wide pastures when she and Navigator ponied Luna. And the big bay stallion had other things on his mind.

Luna was so lovesick over Hoku, one day he inhaled Darby's shirt right into his nostrils. That afternoon, Hoku snapped at the same shirt with such ferocity, Darby began changing clothes between working with the two horses.

Was Hoku the "tomboy mare" that Jonah had called her? Or had Hoku decided not to share Darby? Each day the sorrel filly reflected Darby's affection back to her, and for now, that was most important.

The wild stallion didn't lurk around at daybreak or dusk when she fed Hoku or Francie the fainting goat, or at midnight when she kept watch for him with Cade and Megan on Friday night.

By Saturday, a whole week later, Darby convinced herself he'd taken his herd into hiding, but she couldn't decide if that made it a better or worse time to return the ancient artifact to Crimson Vale.

Of course, she could just keep it here, but it didn't belong to her.

Darby imagined herself swimming in a satin-smooth sea—that would be her perfect life at 'Iolani Ranch—while something dark and octopuslike swirled below her bare legs. That dark threat had something to do with the necklace. She had to take it back to where it had come from.

Giving in to the jump-rope songs Darby chanted, Hoku had accepted the lead rope. Darby could not only lead the filly around; she could actually jump rope while Hoku held her end.

"Not that we'll try that in front of everyone," Darby promised Hoku as she led the golden filly from her corral and out the gate held wide by Megan, for the very first time since her escape.

Kimo, Cade, and Jonah all knew the filly was leaving the confinement of her pen, but they'd agreed with Darby that the best audience for Hoku's premiere would be all girls—Darby and Megan.

The dogs were locked in their kennel. Jonah stood still in the doorway of the tack room. Kimo sat behind the wheel of his truck, ready to give chase if Hoku broke away from Darby. Cade, astride Joker, rode up and down, pretending to check the fence line—but his riata was at the ready. Kit sat astride Kona at the end of the gravel road. If Hoku headed for the street, he'd herd her back to safety.

Darby acted as if it were the most normal of days, and Hoku had nothing to prove to anyone.

"But you'll show them all you're a big girl," Darby teased Hoku.

The filly's flaxen mane and tail floated on an early-morning breeze. Her forelock swept across her brow, showing brown eyes that watched a different world from the one she'd seen through her corral fence.

Hoku raised her tiny muzzle to the height of her neck. She filled her lungs with so much grassy air that when she finally breathed again her exhalation trembled like a baby that had cried itself to sleep.

But the filly danced lively and alert beside Darby, listening to a jump-rope song. Hoku didn't flatten her ears or miss a step when she heard the corral gate close softly behind them, or when Megan's footsteps followed.

Only when they reached the end of the path, climbed the green swell of hill, and descended into the fold between that hill and the next, did the filly grow flighty.

"Shh, girl," Darby said when Hoku gave a single tug at the lead rope.

The filly lowered her golden head, confused for a moment, then became intent on some scent that clung to the grass.

"Yes, Luna's been down here," Darby admitted to the filly, and her eyes slid sideways to catch Megan's.

She'd told her friend that Hoku's aversion to males included the stallion as well as men, and Megan hadn't been very sympathetic.

"I trained Pip to like running with the big dogs," Megan told Darby as she walked on Hoku's right side now. "And that's a lot less natural, since she could be their prey. I'm sure you can do it, after—hey, careful," she warned Hoku as the filly lifted her forefeet from the ground, head swiveling form side to side. "If, I mean, her highness gets over being a drama queen."

"She's not pretending," Darby said, defending the filly. "Hoku was beaten, for sure, and who knows what else. She can't tell me, so I just have to try to figure it out. I think—" Darby's words caught in her throat. Her arms were covered with chills as the filly stopped and stared.

Following Hoku's gaze, Darby saw him. Megan's gasp said she did, too.

The wild stallion stood night-black against the emerald hills. The only part of him that moved was his drifting tail.

"Just turn her around," Megan said softly. "He's not going to follow her back into the corral, and she doesn't act like she wants to go with him."

That was for sure.

With fully flattened ears and eyes narrowed to slits, Hoku glared at the stallion, then at Darby.

"I didn't know what I was getting you into, baby," she told the filly.

Slowly, she tried to turn Hoku back toward her corral, but the filly held her ground.

"I don't blame you, girl. I know he should be the one to leave, but I don't think he's going anywhere while you're out here," Darby told Hoku.

"Stop explaining and get her back inside," Megan snapped. "Here comes Luna."

"What?" Darby reeled with horror, but Luna's

neigh of rage proved Megan right.

And all at once she knew how it had happened. Jonah had told her how easily Luna had hopped over his fence into the weanlings' pen when he was without water.

Now, another stallion was in Luna's territory, within yards of Hoku. The big bay stallion was answering a drive as strong as thirst.

Together, the girls grabbed Hoku's lead rope. One on each side, they held close to her halter as the filly jerked her head up, snorting.

"Just walk away, girl," Megan muttered to the filly. "That's what my mom always says to do with pushy guys."

But they couldn't turn Hoku before the sound of screaming eagles filled the air.

The stallions joined in primitive warnings. Brushing aside mock battle for war, the bay and black reared, forelegs threshing the air before they dropped to all fours and rushed together like knights' chargers.

Chests slammed, necks curved with bared teeth, and both animals drew blood before wheeling to batter each other with slashing, kicking hooves. One bay leg gave way, and then two black ones, but the stallions were evenly matched. The bay was bigger, but the black was swift. Both were up in an instant and neither thought of surrender as they stood panting.

For a minute, Hoku seemed to have lost interest. The girls managed to turn her and drag her toward her corral. It made sense, Darby thought wildly. She'd heard that mares stood idly by, swishing their tails, waiting for the outcome when battles like these happened on the range.

But then Luna and Black Lava were at each other again.

Dust roiled in red clouds. Teeth raked off rows of shining coat.

Any minute, Jonah would be coming with a gun.

Squalls mixed with the pounding of hooves repositioning the horses' heavy bodies for another attack, and Hoku swung around to watch. Her reversal made Darby stumble, but she clung to the orange-and-white lead rope, amazed at the filly's strength.

Hooves struck horseflesh. Hoku snorted. Once, twice, three times, she reprimanded the males. Darby remembered—in wild herds, all the members waited with swishing tails while stallions battled.

Except for the lead mare.

Hoku whinnied. Tossing her head from side to side, she released a sharp neigh that cut through the stallions' fury. The battle faltered. Then it stopped.

When Hoku reared, lifting both girls off their feet, the black mustang shifted his attention to the humans.

The wild horse gazed at Megan and Darby. When Hoku lowered herself back to all fours, the girls crashed down with her. Darby's knees struck dirt and she saw Megan squat, trying to keep her weight low so that Hoku couldn't lift her again.

Neck trembling, the filly gave a final, open-mouthed scream at the stallions. Luna lowered his head and clacked his jaws in apology, but the black stared at her in disbelief.

And then the mustang's attention jerked to another horse running into the field. Cade rode Joker, bearing down on Black Lava with a swinging rope.

Put it away, Darby moaned silently. She knew better than to yell, but oh, how she wanted to. Hoku feared ropes as much as any wild horse. At best, all her work with the filly would be wasted when the filly spooked at Cade's riata.

At worst, Hoku might break free and run away with the wild horse.

The dark stallion feinted right and when the riata flew for his head, the mustang swung left, wheeled on his hind hooves, and launched himself in a black arc to the top of the first knoll.

Luna leaped after him, but the smaller, lighter-bodied mustang had already outdistanced Luna, and Cade had already flung a second loop. This one settled over the mighty bay's head just as Darby heard more hooves thundering behind her.

A blur of speed, Kona streaked past as soon as the bay was caught. Kit had lost his hat and he lay on

Kona's neck as if he were back in the rodeo. Darby had never seen a horse run like Kona did for Kit. The gelding was stretched out like a greyhound, eyes set on the black mustang.

Feeling himself caught, Luna bucked, but he wasn't fighting the rope. He was showing off for Hoku—Darby was almost sure of it.

"Let me at him," Megan pretended to translate Luna's squeals and snorts. "If they hadn't held me back, you'd be dead!" she shouted after the black.

Finally, Luna loped alongside Joker.

Ponying had paid off today, Darby thought, watching the two horses move together.

And her tomboy filly had saved the two stallions from themselves. Although blood dripped from a bite on Luna's neck, he'd escaped serious injury. And the way the black mustang was leading Kit and Kona on a zigzagging chase over 'Iolani's two thousand acres proved he wasn't hurt, either.

After a call from Sun House, Megan jogged there to tell her mother what had happened.

Jonah walked up to check his stallion over, and Luna lowered his head for inspection.

Darby was glad to be alone with her horse.

Now that the excitement was over, the filly trembled. She rubbed her forelock against Darby's chest. Then she sneezed the stallion-raised dust from her nostrils and pulled at the tangerine-and-white-striped rope, leading Darby back to the corral.

"Good girl," Darby crooned to her. "You're right. It's hay time, and you've earned it."

Hoku walked heavy-hoofed, sparing a glance at Jonah, but she didn't shy or spook.

"I guess you told them," Darby whispered to her filly.

Hoku had not only broken up the stallion fight, she'd saved Luna, the ranch's main moneymaker.

Darby glanced at her grandfather to see if he felt as proud of Hoku as she did. He looked up from the cut on Luna's neck and looked over the stallion's gleaming back just long enough to make an "okay" sign with his fingers, and Darby gave a little skip of joy.

Hamburger patties sputtered in an iron pan as Darby, Megan, and Auntie Cathy leaned against the kitchen walls, watching Jonah make them all his favorite big breakfast.

Her mother often cooked hamburgers medium rare and served them on whole-wheat buns for dinner. But Darby could see that Jonah had nothing like that in mind.

In a pan next to the meat, Jonah fried a bunch of eggs sunny-side up, and in the pot next to that, he stirred something that looked a lot like brown gravy.

The rice steamer was plugged in and cooking up what Jonah called sticky rice, too.

Darby had never had hamburgers for breakfast,

let alone all that other stuff, and Jonah must have caught the dubious look on her face, because he laughed.

"Tell you what, Granddaughter," he said, plopping a scoop of rice on a plate. "If you don't like this *loco moko*, there's no hope you'll ever grow up to be a paniolo."

Next, he placed one of the hamburger patties on top of the rice. Atop that, he balanced an egg.

Wide-eyed, Darby said, "I'll like it."

But then, as he ladled brown gravy over everything and handed her the plate, Darby thought cold pizza—the weirdest thing she'd ever had for breakfast up until now—didn't even come close to being this exotic.

Streamers of steam brought all the aromas, plus ginger, up to Darby's nose and she looked at Jonah in amazement.

"It smells wonderful," she told him.

Kimo and Cade would be sorry they'd volunteered to settle Luna down and return him to his pasture if they could smell this amazing dish.

"Dig in," Jonah urged as he made up a second plate for Megan, so Darby did.

It was delicious. They all stood eating in the kitchen, too enthralled with Jonah's creation to make the short walk to the next room, when Kit knocked at the door.

"Come in," Auntie Cathy called.

Holding his Stetson in his hands, Kit stepped inside.

"Sorry to interrupt," he said.

"Nonsense, come have something to eat," Auntie Cathy said.

"No thanks," Kit said. "I've got work, but I thought the boss would like to know Kona and I ran that black stud and his band off the ranch."

"That wasn't the plan," Jonah grumbled.

Darby glanced at Kit, but his expression told her nothing.

"Couldn't get close enough to him to do much else," Kit said, not apologizing or making an excuse, "and his mares were near as fast as he was, so I headed them up toward Two Sisters."

Darby had the feeling that Kit wouldn't have changed the plan if he hadn't been pretty sure Jonah would go along with him.

But then she thought of what Kit had actually said and protested, "That's the opposite direction from their home."

"And steep going," Auntie Cathy put in.

"But maybe they'll be safer up there," Megan pointed out.

Jonah aimed his index finger at her and said, "Mekana's always been quick."

Megan didn't seem to mind Jonah calling her by her Hawaiian name, even though she refused to let Cade do it. But Darby didn't mention the contradiction. Actually, it would have been hard to do, anyway, because she couldn't stop eating her exotic breakfast.

Megan was right, Darby thought as she spooned up a bite of rice. The farther the horses moved away from Manny, the better.

And Kit had made a temporary solution for the ancient necklace possible.

Possible, Darby repeated to herself, *but not probable*.

Before she'd even come to Hawaii, her mother had told Jonah that she was timid, and she was right. Darby wasn't sure she had the nerve to do what she should.

Physically, she could do it. All she had to do now was overcome some really scary thoughts.

"This is against my better judgment," Megan said the next morning as they rode into Crimson Vale.

The dawn sky was silver, pink, turquoise, and as iridescent as the inside of a shell.

Even though the sea was out of sight, far-off waves purred as they washed over the sand.

Darby shivered with anticipation.

"Since you're kind of doing it for me, I won't complain. Much," Megan added, stifling a yawn.

She *was* sort of doing this for Megan, Darby thought, but not really to make amends, as Megan believed.

Darby had known last night, when Hoku was bedded down with extra hay, and Luna had gulped down his bran mash, that she had to make herself do one last thing before she and Hoku left for the rain forest.

Cade had told Darby that Manny was lazy, so Megan had ridden away from 'Iolani Ranch before the smuggler would be up. Once she'd explained the discovery of the *lei niho palaoa* to Jonah, he'd agreed with her idea and promised to make contact with Uncle Kindy, a friend skilled in the sacred ways of old Hawaii.

But Hoku was the one who had challenged two stallions and shown Darby that she had to find the nerve to do this.

Navigator and Conch drew loud breaths as the girls rode through a low-lying cloud that surrounded them with silver mist.

"How about waiting here?" Darby drew rein and prepared to dismount.

"I know it's not my job to be proud of you, but I sort of am," Megan said. "It's cool you understand how I feel about letting the ancestors remain in peace."

"I'll be right back," Darby promised, and Megan leaned over to take Navigator's reins so that she could slip out of her saddle. Actually she fell the last foot to the ground, but she didn't lose her balance. "And this time I mean it."

Megan made a "go on" gesture, as if she didn't even remember the time Darby had fooled her in this place.

Darby had passed a crook in the trail and jumped over a mossy green stream when Megan's faint shout reached her.

"Darby!" Megan shouted. "Watch out for that black mustang. He could have circled back."

"Okay!" Darby yelled, and then she sprinted toward the waterfall.

Darby slowed to a walk, breathing hard and still taking long strides. She watched for the stallion with the sapphire eye. If he'd circled back, she saw no sign of him, but that didn't mean he wasn't hiding in his cave.

That's where she was headed, and when the stallion did return, as she knew he would, he could be the guardian of this precious necklace.

If the stallion was there now, she'd know in a minute.

Pressing herself against the rock wall that held the waterfall, Darby got soaked.

She hadn't meant to. She'd thought she could sneak into the stallion's cave more quickly, but she slipped on foam and ferns before she made it, and then the cave floor slanted down as steep as a playground slide, growing colder with every foot she walked.

Shivering, Darby tried not to think of what might lie ahead.

Hoku hadn't asked herself if she, a delicate two-year-old filly, could break up a fight between two mighty stallions. She'd simply acted as if she could. And she'd done it.

If her horse could take on such a challenge, so could she, Darby thought. She moved on as the cave floor slanted ever more steeply and the damp air pushed into her nose and mouth.

The ancient necklace had traveled with Darby wrapped in a leaf, deep inside her pocket. Darby crab-stepped her way down to the level cave floor. She sighed and stood still, letting her eyes adjust to what she saw.

No way. It wasn't possible that a ring of blackened firewood, turned to charcoal, sat before her. But there it was.

She remembered her dream and for a minute, she let her eyes drift up from the long-dead fire. For the duration of a single heartbeat, Darby thought she glimpsed *things* back there, deeper in the cave behind the waterfall.

She didn't spy on them. It was enough that Jonah had said the bones of her ancestors rested around this ranch. She believed him. She knew some of them slept right here.

If this fragment of jewelry belonged to one of them, she'd brought it home. If not, it would stay in their safekeeping, for now. Bending down, Darby considered a few unburned chunks of driftwood. One piece was smoother than the others and honey-colored. Darby tucked the necklace under it, out of the way of the Shining Stallion's hooves.

I did it, Darby thought as she climbed out of the cave. *All I did was act like I could, and it worked.*

Darby climbed out of the cave, watching dawn's light turn the waterfall into a curtain of gold.

Soaked to the skin, she stepped through it into the sunshine and gazed skyward at a rustling sound. The owl was passing overhead, returning to his ohia tree next to Hoku's corral.

At least that's what Darby decided to believe as she jumped, smiling, back over the green stream and jogged in her squishy boots.

Before Navigator could see her, he neighed, welcoming her, eager to carry her home to 'Iolani Ranch.

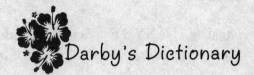

Darby's Dictionary

In case anybody reads this besides me, which it's too late to tell you not to do if you've gotten this far, I know this isn't a real dictionary. For one thing, it's not all correct, and for another, it's not alphabetized because I'm just adding things as I hear them. Besides, this dictionary is just to help me remember. Even though I'm pretty self-conscious about pronouncing Hawaiian words, it seems to me if I live here (and since I'm part Hawaiian), I should at least try to say things right.

'aumakua — OW MA KOO AH — these are family guardians from ancient times. I think ancestors are supposed to come back and look out for their family members. Our 'aumakua are owls and Megan's is a sea turtle.

chicken skin — goose bumps

da kine — "that sort of thing" or "stuff like that"

hanai — HA NYE E — a foster or adopted child, like Cade is Jonah's, but I don't know if it's permanent

'iolani — EE OH LAWN EE — this is a hawk that brings messages from the gods, but Jonah has it painted on his trucks as an owl bursting through the clouds

hiapo — HIGH AH PO — a firstborn child, like me, and it's apparently traditional for grandparents, if they feel like it, to just take hiapo to raise!

hoku — HO COO — star

ali'i — AH LEE EE — royalty, but it includes chiefs besides queens and kings and people like that

pupule — POO POO LAY — crazy

paniolo — PAW KNEE OH LOW — cowboy or cowgirl

lanai — LAH NA E — this is like a balcony or veranda. Sun House's is more like a long balcony with a view of the pastures.

lei niho palaoa — I think that's it—a necklace made for old-time Hawaiian royalty from braids of their own hair. It's totally kapu—forbidden—for anyone else to wear it.

luna — LOU NUH — a boss or top guy, like Jonah's stallion

pueo — POO AY OH — an owl, our family guardian. The very coolest thing is that one lives in the tree next to Hoku's corral.

pau — POW — finished, like Kimo is always asking, "You pau?" to see if I'm done working with Hoku or shoveling up after the horses

pali — PAW LEE — cliffs

ohia — OH HE UH — a tree like the one next to Hoku's corral

lei — LAY E — necklace of flowers. I thought they were pronounced LAY, but Hawaiians add another sound. I also thought leis were sappy touristy things, but getting one is a real honor, from the right people.

luahala — LOO AH HA LA — some kind of leaf in shades of brown, used to make paniolo hats like Cade's. I guess they're really expensive.

kapu — KAH POO — forbidden, a taboo

tutu — TOO TOO — great-grandmother

menehune — MEN AY WHO NAY — little people

honu — HO NEW — sea turtle

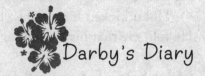 Darby's Diary

Ellen Kealoha Carter—my mom, and since she's responsible for me being in Hawaii, I'm putting her first. Also I miss her. My mom is a beautiful and talented actress, but she hasn't had her big break yet. Her job in Tahiti might be it, which is sort of ironic because she's playing a Hawaiian for the first time and she swore she'd never return to Hawaii. And here I am. I get the feeling she had huge fights with her dad, Jonah, but she doesn't hate Hawaii.

Cade—fifteen or so, he's Jonah's adopted son. Jonah's been teaching him all about being a paniolo. I thought he was Hawaiian, but when he took off his hat he had blond hair—in a braid! Like old-time vaqueros—weird! He doesn't go to school, just takes his classes by correspondence through the mail. He wears this poncho that's almost black it's such a dark green, and he blends in with the forest. Kind of creepy the way he just appears out there. Not counting Kit, Cade might be the best rider on the ranch.

Hoku kicked him in the chest. I wish she hadn't. He told me that his stepfather beat him all the time.

<u>Cathy Kato</u>—forty or so? She's the ranch manager and, really, the only one who seems to manage Jonah. She's Megan's mom and the widow of a paniolo, Ben. She has messy blond-brown hair to her chin, and she's a good cook, but she doesn't think so. It's like she's just pulling herself back together after Ben's death.

I get the feeling she used to do something with advertising or public relations on the mainland.

<u>Jonah Kaniela Kealoha</u>—my grandfather could fill this whole notebook. Basically, though, he's harsh/nice, serious/funny, full of legends and stories about magic, but real down-to-earth. He's amazing with horses, which is why they call him the Horse Charmer. He's not that tall, maybe 5'8", with black hair that's getting gray, and one of his fingers is still kinked where it was broken by a teacher because he spoke Hawaiian in class! I don't like his "don't touch the horses unless they're working for you" theory, but it totally works. I need to figure out why.

<u>Kimo</u>—he's so nice! I guess he's about twenty-five, Hawaiian, and he's just this sturdy, square, friendly guy. He drives in every morning from his house over by Crimson Vale, and even though he's late a lot, I've never seen anyone work so hard.

<u>Kit Ely</u>—the ranch foreman, the boss, next to Jonah. He's Sam's friend Jake's brother and a real buckaroo. He's about 5'10" with black hair. He's half Shoshone, but he could be mistaken for Hawaiian, if he wasn't always promising to whip up a batch of Nevada chili and stuff like that. And he wears a totally un-Hawaiian leather string with brown-streaked turquoise stones around his neck. He got to be fore-man through his rodeo friend Pani (Ben's buddy?). Kit's left wrist got pulverized in a rodeo fall. He's still amazing with horses, though.

<u>Megan Kato</u>—Cathy's fifteen-year-old daughter, a super athlete with long reddish-black hair. She's beau-tiful and popular and I doubt she'd be my friend if we just met at school. Maybe, though, because she's nice at heart. She half makes fun of Hawaiian legends, then turns around and acts really serious about them. She can't stand Cade and he always blushes around her.

<u>The Zinks</u>—they live on the land next to Jonah. They have barbed-wire fences and their name doesn't sound Hawaiian, but that's all I know.

<u>Tutu</u>—my great-grandmother, but I haven't met her yet. I get the feeling she lives out in the rain forest like a medicine woman or something.

❧ ANIMALS! ❧

<u>Hoku</u>—my wonderful sorrel filly! She's about two and a half years old, a full sister to the Phantom, and boy, does she show it! She's fierce (hates men) but smart, and a one-girl (ME!) horse for sure. She is definitely a herd-girl, and when it comes to choosing between me and other horses, it's a real toss-up. Not that I blame her. She's run free for a long time, and I don't want to take away what makes her special.

She loves hay, but she's really HEAD-SHY due to Shan Stonerow's early "training," which, according to Sam, was beating her.

Hoku means "star." Her dam is Princess Kitty, but her sire is a mustang named Smoke and he's mustang all the way back to a "white renegade with murder in his eye" (Mrs. Allen).

<u>Navigator</u>—my riding horse is a big, heavy Quarter Horse that reminds me of a knight's charger. He has Three Bars breeding (that's a big deal), but when he picked me, Jonah let him keep me! He's black with rusty rings around his eyes and a rusty muzzle. (Even though he looks black, the proper description is

brown, they tell me.) He can find his way home from any place on the island. He's sweet, but no pushover. Just when I think he's sort of a safety net for my beginning riding skills, he tests me.

Joker—Cade's Appaloosa gelding is gray splattered with black spots and has a black mane and tail. He climbs like a mountain goat and always looks like he's having a good time. I think he and Cade have a history, maybe Jonah took them in together?

Biscuit—buckskin gelding, one of Ben's horses, a dependable cow pony. Kit rides him a lot.

Hula Girl—chestnut cutter

Blue Ginger—blue roan mare with tan foal

Honolulu Lulu—bay mare

Tail Afire (Koko)—fudge brown mare with silver mane and tail

Blue Moon—Blue Ginger's baby

Moonfire—Tail Afire's baby

Black Cat—Lady Wong's black foal

<u>Luna Dancer</u>—Hula Girl's bay baby

<u>Honolulu Half Moon</u>—Honolulu Lulu's baby

<u>Conch</u>—grulla cow pony gelding, needs work. Megan rides him sometimes.

<u>Kona</u>—big gray, Jonah's cow horse

<u>Luna</u>—beautiful, full-maned bay stallion is king of 'Iolani Ranch. He and Jonah seem to have a bond.

<u>Lady Wong</u>—dappled gray mare and Kona's dam. Her current foal is Black Cat.

<u>Australian shepherds</u>—pack of five and I have to learn their names!

<u>Pipsqueak/Pip</u>—little, shaggy, white dog that runs with the big dogs, belongs to Megan and Cathy

❧ PLACES ❧

<u>Lehua High School</u>—the school Megan goes to and I will, too. School colors are red and gold.

<u>Crimson Vale</u>—it's an amazing and magical place,

and once I learn my way around, I bet I'll love it. It's like a maze, though. Here's what I know: from town you can go through the valley or take the ridge road—valley has lily pads, waterfalls, wild horses, and rainbows. The ridge route (Pali?) has sweeping turns that almost made me sick. There are black rock teeter-totter-looking things that are really ancient altars and a SUDDEN drop-off down to a white sand beach. Hawaiian royalty are supposedly buried in the cliffs.

<u>Moku Lio Hihiu</u>—Wild Horse Island, of course!

<u>Mountain to the Sky</u>—sometimes just called Sky Mountain. Goes up to 5,000 feet, sometimes gets snow, and Megan said there used to be wild horses there.

<u>The Two Sisters</u>—cone-shaped "mountains." A borderline between them divides Jonah's land from his sister's—my aunt, but I haven't met her. One of them is an active volcano. Kind of scary.

<u>Sun House</u>—our family place. They call it plantation style, but it's like sugar plantation, not Southern mansion. It has an incredible lanai that overlooks pastures all the way to Mountain to the Sky and Two Sisters. Upstairs is this little apartment Jonah built for my mom, but she's never lived in it.

<u>Hapuna</u>—biggest town on island, has airport, flag-pole, public and private schools, etc., palm trees, and coconut trees

<u>'Iolani Ranch</u>—our home ranch. 2,000 acres, the most beautiful place in the world.

❧ ON THE RANCH, THERE ARE ❧
PASTURES WITH NAMES LIKE:

<u>Sugar Mill</u> and <u>Upper Sugar Mill</u>—for cattle

<u>Two Sisters</u>—for young horses, one- and two-year-olds they pretty much leave alone

<u>Flatland</u>—mares and foals

<u>Pearl Pasture</u>—borders the rain forest, mostly two- and three-year-olds in training

<u>Borderlands</u>—saddle herd and Luna's compound

I guess I should also add me . . .

<u>Darby Leilani Kealoha Carter</u>—I love horses more than anything, but books come in second. I'm thir-

teen, and one-quarter Hawaiian, with blue eyes and black hair down to about the middle of my back. On a good day, my hair is my best feature. I'm still kind of skinny, but I don't look as sickly as I did before I moved here. I think Hawaii's curing my asthma. Fingers crossed.

I have no idea what I did to land on Wild Horse Island, but I want to stay here forever.

Darby and Hoku's adventures continue in . . .

RAIN FOREST ROSE

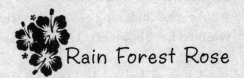# Rain Forest Rose

"Not that it matters, but I've never camped before," Darby Carter told her grandfather, Jonah.

He balanced her backpack behind the saddle cantle, then tightened the knot holding it.

She worried a little bit about her asthma getting out of control, too, but the bulk of the inhaler in her pocket reassured her.

"You want to stay home, say so," Jonah said, but he didn't look at her.

His hands, calloused from decades of work with horses, kept double-checking the job Darby had done saddling up. Now, he tested the breast collar Darby had buckled to keep Navigator's saddle from slipping on steep hills.

"No! I'm going!" Darby insisted.

Her grandfather's smile, which barely lifted the corner of his black mustache, told Darby that he knew her fretting was a habit left over from the noisy school halls, blaring freeways, and city craziness of her life before 'Iolani Ranch.

As the morning clouds parted and sunlight warmed her shoulders, Darby added to herself, *Before Hawaii.*

A low nicker made Darby watch Navigator. The Quarter Horse gelding, dark brown as coffee with rust-colored circles around his eyes, had noticed when she'd glanced down at her pocket. He flared his nostrils, sniffing to find out if she carried something for him in there.

Darby pretended to ignore Navigator, because Jonah didn't like her babying his horses. He'd told her that on her first day in Hawaii. And even though Navigator had picked her as his rider within minutes of her arrival on the ranch, the big gelding still belonged to Jonah.

"Plan on bringing your horse?" Jonah asked.

"Of course," Darby said, but she was thinking, *My horse.*

No other words could kindle a glow inside her like those two.

Well, maybe one: Hoku.

Even though Hoku was a mustang from the Nevada rangelands, Darby had named her sorrel filly

Hoku, the Hawaiian word for "star." She was named for the white marking on her chest but, Darby thought proudly, her horse was a star in other ways. Since coming to Hawaii, the filly had not only braved a long swim in the sea and survived; she'd also chased off a wild stallion set on kidnapping her for his herd.

That first day, Jonah had also told her that the best way to bond with her mustang filly was to set out into the rain forest—alone.

The thought still gave her chills, but so far, everything Jonah had told her about horses had turned out to be true. This morning she would prove she trusted her grandfather as much as he trusted her.

Jonah had given her a map. He'd ride partway out with her to the forest, and then leave her to go on, alone. Astride Navigator and leading Hoku, she'd find the camp marked on the map. It would have a corral for Hoku, a lean-to for Darby to sleep in, and a nearby stream of fresh water. Once she found it, she'd send Navigator home. Then she and Hoku would stay for a week.

We can do it, Darby thought.

"That's good." Jonah faced his own horse now, testing the latigo and buckles on the tack of his gray horse, Kona.

What's good? Darby wondered. The way her mind had darted around, she'd totally lost track of their conversation.

Jonah looked over Kona's back. Brown skin

crinkled at the corners of Jonah's eyes and he tilted his head so that she saw the gray hair at his temples.

At least he didn't look impatient with her, Darby thought, but then she realized her grandfather was gazing past her.

"Here comes the roughrider. Already dropped food out there for you." Jonah gave a wry smile as Cade rode up.

Wearing short leather chaps streaked with green stains, Cade swung in the saddle in time with his horse's high spirits. With his tugged-low hat, rawhide rope, and dark green poncho, Cade looked all business. But not Joker. The black-spattered Appaloosa danced as if he was setting out on an adventure, instead of coming back from one.

"I left your sleeping bag and your food up there," Cade said.

"Good thing he can see in the dark," Jonah told Darby. "Before dawn, that forest is black as the inside of a cow."

"Thanks, Cade," Darby said.

Still in the saddle, Cade shrugged off Jonah's compliment and her thanks.

At fifteen, Cade was only two years older than Darby, but her grandfather's unofficially adopted son was a world of experience ahead of her.

Still, the one thing Darby did best in all the world was learn.

Jonah's eyes flicked toward Hoku's corral. Before

he could rush her, Darby sprinted away.

"I'm getting Hoku. Be right back," she shouted over her shoulder.

As she jogged, Darby took deep, testing breaths. Her asthma had improved since she'd come to Hawaii. Oxygen didn't grate through her lungs and she felt no catch in her chest. The remote island of Moku Lio Hihiu had zero air pollution compared to Southern California.

At the sound of Darby's boots, Hoku bolted away from the fence, then stretched her neck high and higher still to see over the top rail.

"Good morning, beauty," Darby called.

The filly stared through the creamy ripples of her forelock. Sunlight turned her brown eyes amber. She looked as wild as the first day Darby had seen her galloping across a snowy plain, drawing away from the helicopter that had chased her.

"Hoku," Darby said, smooching, and the filly's wild expression was replaced by impatience.

Hoku arched her golden neck and pawed three rapid strokes.

"Were you afraid I was going to leave you behind when I rode out on Navigator?"

Carefully sliding open the new bolt on Hoku's corral, Darby slipped inside, carrying a tangerine-and-white-striped lead rope.

In mock fear, the filly shied away.

Hoku's coat shone with good health. Even though

Jonah said it would take a few more months for the filly to recover from her journey from Nevada to Hawaii, Darby couldn't imagine any horse could be more beautiful.

On her shipping papers, Hoku had been described as a sorrel in one place and a chestnut in another.

To Darby, Hoku looked like living fire. Flashes of flame red outlined the muscles surging beneath the filly's golden skin. Copper glints shone on her legs. Sparks crackled in her flaxen mane.

Hoku stopped, shook her head, and snorted, promising Darby that today she wouldn't be hard to catch.

But Darby had been fooled before, and she didn't have time to calm Hoku if the filly changed her mind.

Darby came to Hoku slowly, with one hand held out to pet the filly if she stepped forward.

She didn't. So, instead of approaching from the front, Darby slid along her horse's side. The filly's body was warm and vibrating with energy.

"Pretty girl," Darby praised, then snapped the lead on Hoku's halter.

Hoku trusted Darby more than she did any other human, but the filly's wild heritage could be traced to horses called "throwbacks" and "renegades." She'd already hurt Cade—out of fear, not malice—and Darby wasn't taking the chance of spooking her horse.

Hoku lifted each hoof in prancing perfection as they moved out of the corral and back toward Jonah.

Her ears tilted forward, curious about the group of people ahead. Even from this distance, Darby recognized her friend Megan by her athletic build and cherry Coke–colored hair, and Auntie Cathy.

Darby had described Auntie Cathy to her own mother as Megan's mom, the resident cook and general ranch manager. But the woman with the messy brown-blond bob was also the widow of a paniolo who'd been Jonah's right-hand man. Auntie Cathy mothered everyone on the ranch, and she knew more about 'Iolani Ranch than anyone except Jonah.

But Hoku wasn't snorting at Megan or Auntie Cathy.

The filly's flattened ears signaled the nearness of a male. She had good reasons to dislike men, and she was warning Cade not to ride any closer.

Cade stopped Joker out of the reach of Hoku's hooves and teeth, but the filly protested with a squeal when Cade leaned down from his saddle to say, "Hope you're not afraid of spiders."

Darby missed a step and tripped into Megan. The other girl steadied her and reached a comforting hand toward Hoku.

"Oh, stop it, Cade," Megan snapped.

"Most of the ones out there are just happy-face spiders." Auntie Cathy dismissed Cade's warning with an indulgent smile.

"Happy-face spiders?" Darby echoed, then looked at Jonah with raised eyebrows.

"No bigger than your little fingernail," Jonah confirmed. When Darby glanced down at her hands, he gave a short bark of laughter.

"They have markings that look like smiles, but they're all a little bit different," Megan explained. Then, hands on hips, she added, "And I think they're cute."

"Not like cane spiders," Cade said in an offhanded manner that contradicted the satisfied expression he'd had when Megan had shuddered.

Darby's first thought was of candy canes, and she said, "They don't sound so bad."

"They're gross. They hide in groves of sugar cane," Megan said, "so you probably won't see them by the corral, but sometimes they migrate. When we were in town once, we saw them march across the street in waves." Megan rubbed her arms with a shudder.

Darby's imagination displayed an undulating carpet of tarantulas, before she could remind herself that she was not afraid of spiders. All creatures were fascinating. She was proud she'd never reacted to snakes and spiders with stereotyped girliness, and she wasn't about to give Cade the satisfaction of seeing her cringe.

"Thanks for the heads-up," Darby told Cade, then tightened her long black ponytail.

At the same time, Hoku stepped closer to her, and Jonah reprimanded, "Keep both hands on that lead rope."

Darby did, and then, before Jonah could tell her to make Hoku back up, she did that, too.

Rules for horses were straightforward and simple with Jonah. If a horse came at you or walked away without permission, you ordered him or her to back up a few steps.

"Back," Darby said, but Hoku just switched her glare from Cade to Jonah, until Darby flicked the end of the lead rope toward the filly's white-starred chest.

Lifting her chin in understanding, Hoku took a step back.

"One more," Darby said and lifted her own chin to acknowledge the filly's response.

"Good," Jonah said. "Now she remembers who's in charge."

"No fair having Hoku stomp them," Cade muttered. "Killing spiders is bad luck."

"So is sleeping with spiders," Megan pointed out, "so shake out your sleeping bag before you bed down every night."

"Enough," Auntie Cathy said, then gave Darby a one-armed hug. "Darby will do just fine."

"Time to go," Jonah said, reining Kona away from them all.

Darby put her boot toe in Navigator's stirrup, but

hesitated before bouncing up into the saddle.

Megan was beside her, whispering, "Let me slip this in here."

"What is it?" Darby asked as Megan unzipped an outside pocket on Darby's backpack.

Megan pushed a small brown sack inside, then zipped it closed again. "Something you can use when you're working with Hoku. It'll get her used to weird things. My dad"—Megan's voice wavered, reminding Darby her friend's father had been dead for only a year—"had me do this with my horse. It worked really well." Megan cleared her throat. "Anyhow, it's fun."

"Thanks," Darby said, then asked, "Which horse?"

For a second, she thought Megan hadn't heard her, but when she started to ask again, Megan said, "Later."

"Promise?" Darby asked, and she wouldn't have noticed Auntie Cathy was following their quiet exchange, except that the woman looked away when Megan rolled her eyes in pretend exasperation, then nodded.

"Watch out for wild pigs," Auntie Cathy put in, as Darby gave Hoku's lead rope one wrap around her hand. "Darby?"

Auntie Cathy's voice was insistent and sharper than usual.

"I'll watch for them," Darby promised. "Even

though I didn't get the pig-tracking class you gave Kit."

"You'll know them when you see them," Auntie Cathy said.

Darby didn't try to analyze the woman's forced lightness.

Jonah was getting ahead of her, so Darby swung into the saddle and nudged Navigator with her heels.

"Bye," Megan called, and Darby looked back over her shoulder to see Cade and Megan wave at exactly the same time.

Darby lifted her reins, telling Navigator to catch up with Jonah as he passed Sun House. The gelding lengthened his stride and Hoku picked her feet up cautiously, following a path of her own, at the end of the tangerine-and-white rope.

As they descended the bluff and crossed the broodmare pasture, Jonah sounded like a coach before a big game, jamming last-minute advice into her brain.

"Work on her head-shyness however you want. You'll build a relationship as you cure the problem," he said. "You've made a start, but halfway won't cut it. It's a dangerous vice. You're goin' nowhere, if you don't fix that."

Hoku didn't have vices, Darby thought. Her head-shyness was a logical reaction to being beaten.

"Down deep, this filly hasn't forgiven you for stealing her freedom."

Don't miss Phantom Stallion: Wild Horse Island #1: The Horse Charmer!

Darby Carter has always loved horses, but as a city girl she's never actually been able to ride. So imagine the thrill when she finds out her grandfather owns a horse farm! In Hawaii! On a tiny island called Wild Horse Island. Could anything be better?

Actually, yes—it turns out that not only will Darby's granddad take her in, he's going to adopt the mustang Darby helped save (in *Phantom Stallion #24: Run Away Home*). So now Darby is off to Wild Horse Island, ready to meet her horse, and begin the adventure of a lifetime...

HarperTrophy®
An Imprint of HarperCollinsPublishers

www.harpercollinschildrens.com